I0537157

Book News

Sign up for exclusive updates and offers at
news.jljarvis.com

The Wanderer

The Wanderer

Highland Soldiers 4

J.L. Jarvis

BOOKBINDER PRESS

THE WANDERER
Highland Soldiers 4

Copyright © 2016 J.L. Jarvis
All Rights Reserved

This book is a work of fiction. Names, characters, places
and incidents are products of the author's imagination or
are used fictitiously. Any resemblance to actual events or
locales or persons, living or dead, is entirely coincidental.
The scanning, uploading and distribution of this book via
the Internet or any other means without the permission of
the publisher is illegal and punishable by law. Please
purchase only authorized electronic editions, and do not
participate in or encourage electronic piracy of copy-
righted materials. Your support of the author's rights is
appreciated.

Published by Bookbinder Press

ISBN (paperback) 978-0-9906476-9-0
ISBN (ebook) 978-0-9906476-6-9

Chapter 1

The Awakening

Isobel Shaw bolted upright in bed as one of the king's royal dragoons flung open the heavy oak door. With a loud thud, it struck the stone wall of the dark bedchamber, and an officer strode to the foot of the bed. Three others came in behind him, one holding a torch.

"By order of the king, Gerard Shaw, your manor and lands are hereby seized."

In the midst of the officer's words, a dragoon pulled her husband out of his bed. When he protested and fought the soldiers, they struck him. The officer gave a nod, and two men dragged Mr. Shaw out of the room and down the stairs.

Of the two who remained, the one giving orders had salted brown hair and an unruffled manner. His strong, wide shoulders and proud stance made him imposing despite his moderate height. Beside him was a tall, young officer with a roguish gaze that made Isobel uneasy.

She looked about for a weapon or means of escape, but there was none.

The shorter man, clearly in charge, spoke gruffly. "Madam, arise and dress yourself."

The younger soldier's eyes traced a leisurely trail from her tousled hair down to her neckline, then to the hem of her thin muslin shift, which was bunched at her knees. Isobel grabbed the disheveled bedcovers and pulled them to her neck.

"If you'd prefer to stay in bed, I'd be happy to accommodate you," said the younger man. He took a step forward, but the other gripped his arm, and he stopped.

Isobel cast alert eyes to the older soldier as she inched back until stopped by the headboard.

"'Tis all right, Madam. You have my word, you are safe." He directed a stern look to the younger soldier, who lowered his eyes, but not before giving Isobel a sly look that sent a frisson of fear through her. Her fate turned on how well the older officer could control the young soldier in his charge.

A loud scuffle on the stairs sent all eyes toward the door.

"Unhand me!" her husband cried out. "They're my stairs, and I'll walk down them myself." Voices and curses rang out, then a series of blunt sounds followed.

The officer in charge sent the younger man to the doorway to see what had happened.

A voice called up to him. "The fool tried to fight us then lost his balance and fell."

"Gerard!" Isobel threw the bedcovers aside and rushed toward the door, no longer caring how she was dressed.

The young officer pivoted around and blocked her

way. He grinned as if it were some sort of cat-and-mouse game. Isobel tried to push past him, but when she tried to rush around to the side of the doorway, the man grabbed hold of her waist to stop her. She struggled, which he took as a chance to put his hands on her—a chance of which he took full advantage. The more she fought him, the more he manhandled her.

It was hopeless to think she would prevail against his formidable strength, but she would not give up. It had never been in her nature to do so, nor would it be now. She did her best to turn back toward the older dragoon. "He's my husband. You must let me help him."

Boots rounded the last few steps at the top of the spiral stairs, and a soldier came into view. "I'm afraid there's no help for him now."

She heard the words but could make little sense of the sounds. Everything seemed to slow down. She knew she should do something, but her head spun, and she couldn't think clearly. Her voice came out in a whisper. "No help for him?"

"It was an accident. He fought us and then lost his balance and fell." He looked plainly at her. "This was not meant to happen."

She trembled as the older dragoon helped her to the edge of the bed, where she started to sit, but then she rose back up and turned to face him. "This was not meant to happen? You barged into our home and pulled my husband out of our bed. And now... are you saying..."

"I'm afraid he's dead. We did not intend—"

She shook her head. "I dinnae care what you intended. My husband is dead, and you killed him!" She slapped him in the face.

The officer barely flinched but gave a nod to one of the soldiers, who came over to pull her away and restrain her.

She could not seem to grasp what was happening. Random moments were flashing through her mind. Remembered voices and phrases rang out through her thoughts. "Why are you here?" she managed to ask one of the officers.

"Madam, why don't you sit down, and we'll bring you some water."

"Sit down and drink water? And what will that do?" She stared at him, first in disbelief, then in anger. "You cannae just barge into people's bedrooms and announce that you're taking their homes—their very lives—from them!"

The officer's voice was quiet and sure. "My dear lady, you'll need to leave now."

"Why? I demand to know why!"

"This is neither the time nor the place to argue the matter."

"It is the perfect time and place. You've barged into my home."

"Madam, we've no time to discuss it."

Anger surged through her as she straightened her back and glared at him. "No time? And yet you found the time to kill my husband. I will ken why, and then I will go to him."

"We were following orders. Any inquiries you have may be addressed to the king."

"I'm addressing you now. I'll not leave without answers."

Two dragoons started to drag her away, but the older

officer held up his palm to stop them. "The king got word of disputes with your tenants," he quietly explained.

"Aye, Mr. Shaw said they were a lazy and ignorant sort who weren't willing to work," she said.

The dragoon's eyes flared in an otherwise expressionless face. "He forced eighty people to live on sixteen acres, from which they were expected to earn rents that amounted to more than your husband himself had to pay. By the time they paid what rent they could, they had nothing left for their families."

She shook her head adamantly. "That cannot be."

"Can it not? Why? Because you don't care for the truth? Have you ever visited your tenants?"

Isobel searched for words. "Our wedding was but two weeks ago. Mr. Shaw was going to take me out soon to meet all the tenants."

"Was he? Mistress Shaw, this has gone on for too many years. Last month, your husband raised the rent once again, to three times what he paid for his lands. There were rumblings of the farmers banding together like they have elsewhere in Scotland. King James has had his fill of uprisings—first the Covenanters, and now the farmers—so he's putting a stop to it. For a start, he is seizing your house and your lands."

She looked quizzically at him. It was all too much to absorb. She felt numb.

"Do you understand what I am saying?" the officer asked. "Your tenants could never have paid what they owed and provided for their families."

Isobel peered at him, stunned. "Mr. Shaw would not have done such a thing."

"Children were starving," he said with quiet restraint.

Isobel thought of the day her husband brought her home. Everyone they'd passed—the workers on the grounds and in the house—had all watched them with silent respect... or just silence. The children were starving?

"May I see him?"

Stepping aside, the dragoon led her to the small spiral staircase, staying closely behind her lest she lose her footing on the stone steps. At the bottom, she knelt beside her husband's lifeless body and smoothed the gray strands from his brow. For a long while, she sat with him as if he might awaken, even though she knew well he would not.

All her anger was gone, replaced by numb confusion. Whoever this man was, and whatever he had done, he was her husband. She could not leave him here as they'd ordered. Her voice came out in a whisper. "He must be buried. I've never done this before. I dinnae ken what to do."

"We'll take care of it, Mistress Shaw." Isobel looked at the older dragoon. Behind his soldier's reserve, she saw a hint of compassion. Of course, he had buried the dead many times and would know what to do. Given his age, which appeared to be older than the others around him, she wondered at how he would feel anything, having served so many years and having killed so many people.

Men of conscience must have to come to terms somehow with their actions. Acting with honor must be the only way to guard against guilt. Regardless of why, she was strangely grateful for his assistance in burying her husband, even though his own men were the cause of his death.

Isobel felt lost. The king's men were seizing not only

the house and the land, but everything on it, livestock included. They had taken her home and her husband, and she feared he had brought it upon them. Had he treated his tenants fairly, would any of this have happened? Even if their home would have been seized either way, had her husband not struggled against the soldiers on the stairs, would he be alive now?

But choices had been made, and actions had been taken, and now Isobel was the only one left to suffer the consequences. The only choice she had made was to marry the man who had brought this upon them—the man whom she thought would provide her that secure and calm life she had hoped for. Now she had nothing. She could do nothing. How could a woman alone fight an army of men or the king whom they served?

She could not. So she buried her husband and set out on foot for her family's home with what few coins and jewels she had been able to hide and sew into her skirt hem. How she would get home was something she dared not think about, for although she had made the trip here from the Highlands, she had not had to worry which way the horses were going. But now she had only the sun to guide her, along with what guidance she might get from strangers along the way—or what harm she might receive. Thinking too much about that wasn't going to help, so she fixed her mind on what needed attention at the moment.

"You wanted to be in charge of your own life. Here you are. One foot after the other, and don't you dare shed one tear."

Chapter 2

The Escape

After a long day's ride from Edinburgh, Charlie MacDonell had not expected to find such an eager companion, nor—truth be told—had he sought one. But late into the night, as he sat in an oak-paneled corner of an inn and finished what he'd decided would be his last tankard of ale, he looked up and saw not quite an angel, but close enough at this hour, leaning over the banister, plump mounds pushing free from her stays as she leaned her folded arms on the dark oaken banister above.

She smiled down upon him, not quite like an angel. No angel looked down at a man with such warmth or less virtue, and although he had recalled seeing her arrive on the arm of a man who was no doubt her husband, she was clearly alone now and even more clearly in search of, well, him.

He liked a woman who knew what she wanted. Who was he to deny her? So he met her gaze and offered an agreeable grin before he finished his tankard of ale with a swig, set it down, and walked outside. Minutes later, the door of the inn scraped open, and a shadowy form slipped outside, taking a few steps before stopping.

"'Tis a bit late for a walk." Charlie fixed his gaze firmly upon the woman as he leaned against a large tree, arms folded.

"Oh, aye, 'tis very late—for a walk, but a walk was not what I was wanting." In spite of the darkness, it took her no time to make her way toward him. By the time she stopped talking, her warm breath brushed his neck, and her lips were on his. Her body was plump in the places he liked it to be. There were moments in life that were good.

What was not good was falling asleep in the hay, which they did sometime later.

A MAN's voice cut through the dawn stillness as an inn door slammed closed. Charlie and his curvy companion sprang into action, sorting through items of clothing. Charlie leapt onto his horse and ducked down to clear the top of the byre door. He maneuvered his way past the oncoming innkeeper's wife, who hopped out of his way, nearly spilling her basket of eggs.

"Eh, sir!" she angrily called after him.

The young woman emerged from the door to the byre behind him. She watched him while tucking her ample bosom back into her stays. A breeze caught straight strands of Charlie's dark-blond hair as he glanced back to flash a broad grin at the woman, unfazed by the irate man that followed him. Charlie assumed the man was her husband, dressed only in his léine. After two attempts, the man mounted a horse and gave chase, silver curls wildly bobbing like loose springs above a nose that resembled a barely ripe strawberry. But by then, Charlie was well on his way, while the galloping horse hooves behind him grew distant.

His eyes lit to recall it even as he outrode his pursuer. He tilted his head, and a crooked grin formed. *Well, we all make mistakes.* Past mistakes came to mind in a series that could have gone on had he not dismissed them with a groan. For as much as he might have enjoyed what was now a long list of women he'd had the great pleasure of knowing, the same nagging emptiness threatened his peace. It never used to trouble him, but as the years had passed, he'd found himself wondering if there ought not be more to his life.

His friends Callum, Duncan, and Alex had found their true loves, and they had gone on and on about how love had bettered their lives. It wasn't that they weren't convincing, nor was he against the idea completely. He just didn't seem to be able to feel it.

And then there was the way that love—all love, even the non-romantic variety—ended. People left, people died, and it hurt when they did. Why invite it? No, he had the best life. It was simple and easy. If there were women about, there were women to bed. Of course, there were times in between when he sometimes felt empty—increasingly empty—but Charlie was usually able to shake off the feeling, which he did then.

HIS TRUSTED STEED had been pounding the turf for the good part of a day when a thick Scots mist rolled in and settled over the land. Charlie loosened his thighs' grip against his horse and leaned back in the saddle, taking time to advance over the fog-covered terrain. He'd traveled this route many times, and yet even the most familiar land became strange when obscured by a mist. The rush of water drew him toward his goal. There was a cave he had found in his travels by chance one summer night, not far from a small waterfall. If he followed the sound, there was a chance he might find it. He got down off his horse and walked with some care, for beyond an arm's length, he could see nothing but fog. Still, he pressed on. If he failed to find it, he would have to settle for a hidden spot in some foliage, where he might be rained on. Either way, his horse needed rest, and Charlie wouldn't mind some sleep, either. He would be up before the air cleared, surely well on his way before anyone found him.

He thought he'd drawn close to the cave when his ears perked. He could hear water tripping over the rocks very faintly at first, and then louder. The ground softened. Then the mist cleared for a moment, and he saw it. Beyond the dark opening of the cave, shelter and safety awaited. After leaving his horse by the stream, Charlie went inside. Having had little sleep, for reasons he did not entirely mind, he now found himself feeling weary, indeed. His mouth quirked at the corner. Aye, she'd been worth it. Still, while he had no regrets, he looked forward to closing his eyes for a bit. With the thick mist outside, he felt as safe as one could hope to be while alone in the wild.

Something hard pressed against his back.

He stiffened and lifted his hands. "I'm sorry. If it's gold that you want, I've got none." His instinctive charm warmed the sound of his voice, or so he hoped. "I'm on my way home from a card game. If you hurry back to the inn, you might find its new owner. He's about so tall, a bit round in the middle, with gray curly hair."

The gun barrel pressed harder into his neck.

"You're welcome to search me. I've naught for you. I'm sorry."

After a lapse, his assailant spoke. "On the ground. Face down. Now!" A toe kicked his leg—well, his boot. Charlie didn't mind the kick, but the voice drew his notice. It was high. His attacker was no more than a boy. Charlie turned his ear toward his assailant. "On the ground?" he asked with as much innocence as he could muster.

"Of course on the ground. Are you daft?"

"Oh, aye. All right, then." He complied, getting down on his knees, and then with a swift turn, he hooked his arms about the thief's ankles and yanked his feet out from under him. With a thud and a grunt, the lad fell. Charlie climbed onto him, gripped his hand, and wrestled a pistol from an unexpectedly delicate hand. Long hair caught in his hands as his would-be captor fought back, thrashing about until Charlie's hand grasped hold of surprising evidence that his attacker was, in fact, not a boy but a woman. She cried out and tried to bite his arm, but he snatched it away before she could clamp her teeth onto his wrist.

"I'm sorry. I thought you were a lad, but I see—or feel, rather, that you are not." Through the dim light in the cave, he peered at her.

She thrashed about. "Well, now that that's settled, would you kindly get off me?"

Charlie had too much honor not to comply but was

rewarded with elbows and knees jabbed in uncomfortable places as the woman sprang toward the mouth of the cave.

Caught off guard, Charlie fumbled his way up and lunged for her, knocking her down. "God's teeth, woman!" But his anger defused as he breathed in her lavender scent.

"You're a fine-smelling thief." He lay over the length of her body, this time making no attempt to move. Instead, he examined the pistol she held then rolled his eyes.

"I'm no thief." Her voice betrayed her fear as she struggled beneath him.

His mouth turned up at the corner. "Oh? Well, threatening me with this—as it turns out—unloaded pistol suggests otherwise."

"You came into my cave," she said with an edge to her voice.

"Did I? Your cave, is it?" Charlie's eyes swept over her. Now that they were at the mouth of the cave, enough light shone in to see his assailant. Although not the most beautiful woman he'd seen, she was pretty enough. And, since forced to, he didn't mind lying on top of her nicely shaped figure.

She ignored his assessing gaze. "I was here first."

"Aye, so you were. The question is why?"

"I owe you no explanation!"

Charlie grinned. "Well, dearie, since you're the one on the bottom, then I'd say you owe me whatever I ask for."

That sparked a new struggle from her and a good laugh from Charlie, for she was no match for his strength. While he did not object to her writhing, it was not in his nature to wrestle young ladies—unless they were willing, which this one clearly was not. Just as he was loosening his grip to release her, she managed to scratch him on the neck. Charlie cursed and looked up at the ceiling as he let out a deep sigh. Quickly tiring of this game, he made quick business of pinning her wrists to the ground. "You'd best stop hurting me, before I hurt you."

She writhed beneath him. "As if stopping would change that!"

"What do you mean? I'm defending myself! What kind of a blackguard do you think I am? I'd not harm you on purpose." Having at last pinned her down with no hope of escape, she ceased struggling, much to Charlie's relief, for it took more energy than he cared to expend just to avoid hurting her. "God, where did you learn to fight like this?"

"Older brother."

"Well, God help him."

"Oh, he did. But he left me alone. No sense wasting God's help on a woman." She spoke quietly, but her voice sounded tense. A fleeting sadness came into her eyes and was gone just as quickly.

Charlie sighed and spoke gently. "Well, dearie, I'm sorry."

She snarled. "I don't need your pity."

Charlie's kindness was, it seemed, wasted on her. Still, he could not help but be intrigued by her plight. Ill-equipped as she was to prevail against him—and he was more gallant than most she would likely encounter—it seemed increasingly apparent to Charlie that she had not found herself there by choice. And that was what intrigued him. Why, then, was she there? "From the sound of it, you've had a hard life."

She scoffed. "Hard? No. I've had everything handed to me, including—" She stopped and looked away. "'Tis no business of yours."

"It became my business when you poked that pistol into my back."

"Did it?" Her voice was as smooth as syrup. "Well, I'm sorry. I meant to offer you tea, but I couldnae find the tea service here in this cave."

Charlie laughed and began to relax. "I'll make a deal with you. I'll not harm you—nor ask for tea—if you'll promise the same."

"Oh, you want me to trust you? And why should I do that?"

"Because I'm the one holding you pinned to the ground. I could have done anything I wished, but I haven't—which is not to say that a thought or two didnae cross my mind—but I've done nothing improper, nor will I." He looked frankly into her eyes, prompting her to look anywhere but at him.

A long silence followed.

"Lass, did you hear me? I said that I'll not harm you if you promise the same."

She let out an exasperated sound. "Very well."

"Very well—what?"

"Very well, I'll not harm you, either."

He looked into her eyes with a serious frown. "Or make tea?"

"Or make tea." Charlie felt sure he caught an amused glint in her eyes, but she held firm to show her strength—of character only, for she was too lithe to pose any real sort of a threat, provided he kept his gunpowder away from her pistol.

In light of her vulnerable bargaining position, he found her dogged spirit endearing, though he would not disclose that to her. Remembering himself, he released her. "All right."

A glimmer of sunlight streamed into the cave and cast a sheen on the thick, deep-brown hair that cascaded over her shoulders and down to her waist. The sight nearly made him forget how she vexed him. Her dark eyes locked intently on his, and against all good sense, he had an impulse to kiss her. Averting what would have been a terrible error in judgment, he stepped aside and offered a bow. "Good day, madam."

She said nothing.

Charlie raised an eyebrow as he turned and walked away. When he got to his horse, he paused with his hand on the saddle. *Get on your horse, man, and ride away. Dinnae look back.*

He looked back.

There she was, where he'd left her, just looking at him, her forehead wrinkling.

Once more, he turned, ready to mount his horse and ride off, but he didn't. He exhaled then turned back and studied her for a moment. "Well, I cannae leave you there all alone."

She lifted her chin with a grand show of pride that he doubted she genuinely felt. "Why not? I can take care of myself."

"I'm sure that you can. Where are you going?"

"None of your business."

"Aye, you're right." He put his foot in the stirrup and hoisted himself into the saddle. He'd wasted enough of his time on this woman.

"Fort William."

He turned back toward her, brow creased.

She lifted her chin.

"You're not a Cameron, are you?" He'd spent a good deal of time fighting Covenanters for the previous king. With the killing times freshly behind the people of Scotland, the last thing he wished was to have any dealings with Cameronians.

"No, I am not."

He wasn't at all sure he believed her, but with intermittently volatile tension between clans, he wouldn't blame her for concealing the truth. If she were a Cameron, it might even work to his advantage. Helping her might buy him safe passage through Cameron country.

She grew impatient with the brief silence between them. "If you'll just tell me the way to Fort William... Does this road go straight there?"

His eyes sparkled with amusement she did not share. "That depends upon how you define straight."

"If I stay on this road, will it take me there?"

"It might, but your feet are another matter entirely." With a dismissive glance at her silk slippers, he took a step toward her, but she quickly stepped backward and glared at him.

Color flushed her cheeks. "Thank you for your opinion, but you've no idea what I am capable of."

"I'm beginning to." His slight smile drew a frown from her.

"Just answer my question," she said.

Charlie was tempted to do just that and be on his way. He'd already spent enough time with this woman. Any gentlemanly obligation he might have had to her clearly ended about the same time she'd scored his neck with her fingernails. And yet one look at her made it clear to him that she would not last long alone in the rugged Highlands. Even at this time of year, the conditions were harsh. She might have the clothing and speech of a woman who had means and education, but he would wager she had not spent one day in the Highlands—or Lowlands, for that matter—on her own, sleeping under the stars.

His horse grew restless. "I ken how you feel," he muttered to his horse as he gave it a gentle pat on the neck. Charlie exhaled, annoyed, for he couldn't leave her to her inevitable demise. While it was true that she'd tried to assault him, albeit with an unloaded pistol, she was merely defending herself against a stranger who, had it been someone else, might have harmed her. While, to his embarrassment, she had gotten a few kicks and scratches past his defenses, she posed no real threat to him. Still, he had questions.

"What brought you here, Mistress?"

"Oh, I see. I asked you a question—a simple one, really—and you think that entitles you to pry into my life. Well, I thank you for your time, sir." And with that, she tromped off toward the road.

God's teeth, why did this woman irritate him so? Charlie gave up searching for an answer that did not include a curse. Instead, he just sat atop his horse and watched her ungracefully maneuver through the rough terrain in her flimsy silk slippers, which were pitiably ill-equipped for the job. Given her abrasive manner, he'd earned the bit of entertainment this provided for having put up with her these past minutes—or had it been hours? It surely felt like it.

Charlie lingered behind long enough for her to walk off her foul mood. When she'd gone well out of sight, he followed on horseback. Her head turned only slightly at the sound of his approach. Charlie passed her by and brought his horse to a stop before her. "Get on." It was not a request.

She came to a halt and stared past him. He could almost hear each thought as it went through her head. When she seemed to have arrived at her only feasible choice, he reached down and offered his hand.

Her eyes clouded as her determination and pride faltered. She stoically lifted her chin. "I've no wish to trouble you further. I'll be fine on my own." Then she whispered, "God willing."

Charlie shook his head. "Lass..."

She kept walking. He was beginning to think she was stubborn enough to refuse him no matter what he might say, so he rode up ahead and stopped, blocking her path once again. His gaze bore through her. "I'll not let you go on alone to your death."

That got her attention. Charlie's eyes softened. "Nor will I harm you."

She eyed him for a long time before she reluctantly gave a slight nod. Gripping his hand, she used his flexed boot as a step while he pulled her up behind him.

"Hang on."

Chapter 3

Safe Journey

Those were the last words they exchanged until after they'd stopped to rest the horse. The sound of rushing water guided them off the road to a stream otherwise hidden by a surrounding thicket of trees.

On a patch of thick moss, Charlie knelt down and splashed water on his face, then took several drinks with cupped hands before stretching out on the grass and closing his eyes. There he lay, breathing in the pungent aroma of moist soil and decayed branches and leaves that a wild Scottish wind had tossed about.

"My name's Charlie MacDonell." When she did not reply, he opened one eye. She was seated well out of reach, naturally, but still within earshot. "Mistress, have you a name?"

"Isobel Shaw."

"'Tis a pleasure to meet you, Isobel."

"Mistress Shaw."

"Of course. Forgive me. I've been at war too long and

have forgotten my manners." The women he visited seldom had last names.

"That's quite all right, Mr. MacDonell." She closed her eyes, putting an end to the discussion.

Charlie was torn from drowsy bliss not a quarter of an hour later by a cry from a short distance off.

"Mistress Shaw?" She was where he'd last seen her, sitting up, looking frightened and a little confused.

With a start, she turned toward him. "Yes?" She brushed off her skirt and stood up. "Are we leaving, then?" She almost looked as though nothing had happened until she nervously cast her eyes away.

There was something not quite right. "Are you well?"

She readily nodded.

Her notably agreeable manner, which he had not experienced since their acquaintance, confirmed his suspicions that something was amiss. What it was, though, he could not determine. "From the sound of your cry, I was sure you'd been injured."

Once more, she looked away rather than meet his eyes. "I... had a bad dream."

"'Tis no shame in that." He brushed off bits of leaves and twigs that still clung to his plaid after his earlier nap. "Well, it's over. I'll finish filling the waterskin, and we'll be on our way."

THE SUN CAST long shadows over the braes and down into the glen. He had not seen so many shades of green since he'd left home. That and the scent of wild Highland grasses and flowers brought memories that gripped his heart. Memories of people soon followed. So many most dear to him were now gone. He shook off those thoughts.

"Are you feeling better, Mistress Shaw?"

"I am, thank you."

She sounded as though she'd been about to tell him something different but then changed her mind. He still knew nothing about her. What caused a woman of her apparent social stature to be left alone on a roadway? Whatever it was, she had no intention of sharing it with him. That much was clear. Why he bothered to wonder was less clear. He was doing the honorable thing by getting her safely to—well, that was another question. No matter, he was acting with honor, which he feared he'd forgotten how to do. Still, he wondered.

"Mistress Shaw, what brought you to a cave by the roadway?"

She sighed. "The king's men, if you must know."

Charlie was glad she was riding behind him and couldn't see him frown as he speculated as to the reasons the king's men might have abandoned her on the road. None were good. He did not have to wonder for long.

"I awoke yesterday to find royal dragoons at the foot of our bed—my husband's and mine. They pulled him from me and said that the king was thereby seizing our home, our land, and everything on it. They dragged him to the stairway and, as they were taking him downstairs, something happened. They told me he fell. Perhaps he did, or perhaps he was pushed. I'll never be certain. I just know that, in that moment, I lost everything. They at least had the decency to bury him for me before they turned me out of my home. They didn't have the decency to leave me a horse." She paused to take in a breath. "I set off down the road in the direction I'd come from on my wedding day. I'd walked half a day when I found the cave where we met."

"I'm sorry." He nearly told her that he had known loss, but that would have invited discussion. Although he was moved by her plight, he was not ready for that conversation.

It had been more than four years since his brother had died, and he still had moments when he wondered how Hugh would react to something that had happened. And then he would remember that Hugh was gone. He could not yet control his reaction to such thoughts, so he found it best to avoid them.

Lost in their separate ruminations, Charlie and Isobel rode on in silence until she sighed. He looked back over his shoulder and was met with her warm brown eyes. Every time she looked directly at him like that—and she had done so a few precious times—he felt a moment's twinge of emotion. His twinges, where women were concerned, usually occurred somewhat south of his heart, so this new sensation baffled him. His smooth tongue and piercing blue eyes had served him well over the years, leaving him in control—and he liked it that way. But this woman's soft gaze disarmed him.

He refocused his thoughts. "There's a forest ahead. If there's water nearby, we'll stop for the night."

THERE WAS INDEED WATER, as well as a pheasant, which Charlie roasted over a fire. He was pleased to see Mistress Shaw devour her portion, for she looked a bit thin and drawn. Now that she'd had a good meal, all she needed was some sleep.

They lay side by side, looking up at the sky. It was unusually clear, with brilliant pinpricks of light scattered across the velvety swath of blackness. The moon was so full, it cast an enchanted light on the gently sloping land all about them.

"When was the last time you saw such a sky?" Mistress Shaw asked.

"A long time ago." Catching himself feeling wistful, Charlie changed the subject. "You said you'd walked half the day from your home when I found you?"

"Aye, they took me down the road and then left me. I suppose they didnae want me to find my way back and cause trouble."

Charlie nodded, pleased that he'd earned enough trust for her to actually answer a simple question. So, while she was in the mood to talk, he pressed her for more details.

"Did they say why?"

"We'd only been married two weeks. I'd asked to meet the tenants, but Mr. Shaw said it was not a good time. He said they were ungrateful and angry, but the soldiers told me my husband was charging three times what he ought to for rent, and the tenants were close to revolting."

Charlie exhaled. So her husband had been a greedy lout who would have stopped at nothing to build his own coffers at the expense of his tenants. That bit of information had painted enough of a portrait of Mr. Shaw to convince him that, despite the man's unfortunate death, Charlie would not have liked him.

Mistress Shaw went on. "He was well within his rights to set the rents, but there were eighty people trying to make a living from sixteen acres of land. I never knew. Those poor people were starving. There was talk of them banding together. But when Mr. Shaw turned out a family who had just paid their rent, for the sole purpose of having the croft for his own use when he fished the nearby river, word got to the king, and he intervened."

Charlie nodded. No doubt the newly crowned King James had seen enough Covenanter uprisings to want to avoid further unrest. And this was just the sort of situation that could set off a rebellion.

Mistress Shaw let out a rueful chuckle.

In the dark, Charlie could not gauge her expression enough to know how he should react.

As if reading his thoughts, she said, "Dinnae worry. I've not lost my mind. Or if I have, it happened the day I agreed to marry Gerard Shaw."

Charlie trod lightly. "People do things for love." Not that he would know. He had never been in love in his life. He'd long ago accepted the fact that he could not fall in love. His friends all had, leaving him like a poor wandering soul with his nose pressed to the glass.

"I'd not known him long enough to feel love," Mistress Shaw said. "He presented himself to my brother and asked for my hand. When my brother informed me, we argued. He reminded me that I was almost too old to marry."

Charlie let out a laugh. "Oh, I think you might have a few good years left in you." He'd managed to steal a few appraising looks over the course of their day together. "You can't be more than two and twenty." The awkward silence that followed caught him off guard.

"Six and twenty."

Charlie smiled. "God's wounds! A year older than I. You are ancient!"

The edge in her voice did not sound like amusement. "'Tis different for men. And that was what angered me so when he said it. He was right. All my life, I've been subject to different rules. I've watched him ride off for exciting adventures while I stayed in the solar and perfected my needlework. When our father died, John got everything, including our home. I had nothing. Nor was I, apparently, welcome to stay at home for long. So I thought, if I married, I'd be the mistress of my own house. For the first time, I'd have some control over my life."

Charlie had never thought of how it must have been for the girls. He'd always thought they enjoyed their lot as much as he enjoyed his.

She looked away. "Och, I dinnae ken why I'm telling you this."

"Because I asked, and I'm interested." And he was—to a point that surprised even him.

"Oh, aye. Well, you're either very polite or a shameless flatterer."

"Are those the only two choices?"

She studied him. "I'm leaning toward one."

He was fairly sure he knew which. He was not proud to hear it, and yet in truth, he was worse than anything she might think to call him. For years, he'd been running away. When his clansmen went home after fighting Covenanters, he'd gone off to fight elsewhere—not for honor or what he believed in, but for anyone who would pay him. He gave away his Venetian red British uniform coat and sailed to Sweden to serve as a soldier of fortune. He'd had no intention of wearing it again and was glad to

be rid of it. But he soon found himself with some inter-
esting—and sometimes unsavory—sorts. But they were all
there for their own separate reasons. As long as they left
him alone, he had no quarrels with them. He was there for
the fight. He didn't much care who or what he fought for,
as long as they paid him. But a few years of it had darkened his soul. He'd lost track of the honor and pride he
once felt when fighting with his clansmen.

"You're quiet," Mistress Shaw said. "Are you fashing
about what I said?"

"What? Och, no. I was just thinking."

"Polite."

He'd been nearly asleep, but he managed a groggy,
"Hmm?"

"The one choice—I think you're very polite."

He lifted an eyebrow. "Oh, Mistress Shaw, you're a
fine judge of character." *The poor woman.* He settled back
down to sleep.

MORNING SUN CAST a silvery hue to the mist that
hovered close to the ground. Charlie opened his eyes and
discovered he was alone. "Mistress Shaw?" When no
answer came, he waited and listened. He called out again.
Stepping away was no cause for alarm, but not answering
was. As he prepared to go search, he imagined what sort of
harm might have befallen her. Then footsteps announced
her approach, and he relaxed—so much so that it signaled
the depth of his concern. He was borrowing trouble by
worrying, when that was the very thing he had spent five
years fleeing. Today's worry would, in time, be a future

regret, and he had enough of those. All he wanted was to leave all those feelings behind him and go home.

"Aye, Mr. MacDonell?"

Her voice sounded much closer than he'd expected, and Charlie turned just as Mistress Shaw tripped on a tree root and flew straight at him. He cursed as the force threw them both to the ground. She landed on top of him, and they lay face-to-face. Charlie looked up and flashed a wicked grin. "Well, dearie, it looks like you've got me where you want me. Now what shall we do?"

A slap in the face would have been understandable, but he did not expect a firm punch to the side of his nose. She scrambled to her feet, shaking her hand as if doing so would rid it of the pain, then she cradled it to her chest while she moaned.

He, in turn, forced back most of the curses that burned to be spoken. Drops of blood fell from his nose and interrupted his sputtering. He stared at her in disbelief. "Why, you've bloodied my nose, ye wee— Och! I'm not used to cursing at women. I cannae even think one. But you'd deserve every word if I could!"

With no warning, she laughed.

"Oh, you find that amusing?" Charlie held part of his plaid to his nose and glanced sideways at her, nonplussed. But her laugh was contagious. He nearly joined in, for this was something he understood. Granted, sharing a laugh with a woman usually came with a lusty roll in the hay with an agreeable lassie. And then, just as quickly, she stopped.

She didn't cry. Had she done so, he wouldn't have blamed her, although he wouldn't have enjoyed it, either. But she just looked away with as stoic a face as he'd seen on a person—man or woman. Her voice was quiet but sure. "I'm sorry, but you angered me."

"So I gathered." Charlie frowned as he turned away and kept the rest of his thoughts—and the blood from his nose—to himself.

"I think it would be best if we parted ways." Mistress Shaw turned and started to leave, but he grasped hold of her wrist.

"And just where are you going?" He followed her gaze to his hand on her wrist and let go.

She bowed her head. "To my home. And I wish you a safe journey to yours."

Charlie balked. "Oh, do you? Well, I wish you one, too, which is why I'll not leave you alone, not to mention on foot." He rolled his eyes then fixed them on hers. "You're coming with me."

Her troubled gaze moved him, which prompted him to abruptly turn from her and stride to his horse. He wiped the last bit of blood from his nose and, with a wave of his hand, invited her to mount his horse.

She hesitated.

Until now, he might have wished her good luck and pointed her in a safe direction as he rode off in another. But he could not seem to leave her. Whether from shock or lack of better options, she appeared oddly calm. Perhaps she no longer cared for her safety, and perhaps he did. For whatever reason, a thin thread of understanding linked them together.

Light caught her soft brown eyes. "Are you sure?"

To conceal how much he appreciated the light in her eyes, he lowered his gaze past her smooth cheekbones and soft lips. His voice sounded more tender than he had intended. "Aye, I'm sure."

He frowned at the ground. What now? Was he actually feeling awkward with a woman? He was not himself. He resolved to regain what was left of his senses and tilted his head toward the saddle. "Come, dearie... uh, Mistress Shaw."

Through her otherwise expressionless face, he caught a glimpse of pain in her eyes, and it tugged at his heart. He didn't know what to make of her. She was stubborn and strong, but in that one glimpse, he saw that something was broken. *Of course it is, you toad,* he derided himself. *She has just lost her husband.*

Logic told him it was not too late to move on and leave her behind, instead of pulling her into his tender embrace until the ache in her eyes faded away. But he knew himself too well to believe that his good intentions would rule over desire. He would want in return, and if offered, he would take. He was not proud to admit it, but he knew himself far too well to imagine another outcome. He'd been cursed with a deep affection for women, and they had an innate sense of interest in him.

Given the least indication, he had never been good at resisting. And yet he was doing that now—for the time being. The thought of bedding her had crossed his mind, but he was as good as poison for Mistress Shaw, and he knew it. Perhaps she knew it, too. Even if she had not just lost her husband, she was not the sort who could take such things lightly. He had learned early on that her sort —the serious ones—tended to complicate things, so it was best to avoid them.

Charlie stepped aside and offered his hand to help her mount his horse. "Shall we?"

As she took his hand, Mistress Shaw's foot caught on her skirts, and she stumbled into his arms. Charlie looked up to the heavens and wondered why God would test him so. Here she was, leaning on him and grasping hold of his forearms to steady herself. Her loose wisps of hair struck his hands like silk lashes as she bent down to pull her skirts free, and he smelled the faint, sweet scent of bog myrtle. Her clothing was caught on something, and she tugged with increasing frustration.

"Easy, lass, you'll tear it." He bent down to assist, but his face came too close to hers. Startled by the sudden proximity, she stood up too quickly and reached for the saddle to steady herself, but she missed. A slight hop brought her close enough to grab hold of the saddle. But the horse responded to her movement and shifted its weight. She was toppling over when Charlie's strong hands grasped her waist. When she was securely righted, Charlie let go and knelt down, spying the source of the trouble. She was standing on a branch, the opposite end of which was caught in her skirt hem. With a firm yank, he freed it, affording him a glimpse of her ankle and calf. Mere inches away, his fingers were so close, he could touch the soft skin by mistake—or by impulse. As he pondered how soft she would feel to his touch, she stepped away and smoothed down her skirts.

Charlie cursed himself for the vile rogue that he was before mounting his horse. He pulled Mistress Shaw up behind him and rode away.

IT WAS NEARLY dark when they stopped for the night. Warmed by the fire on this cool summer night, they supped on fresh salmon in comfortable silence. When they finished, Charlie offered his flask of whisky. Mistress Shaw took a dainty sip, which drew a laugh from Charlie.

"Sorry, lass, but you'll have to do better than that." He proceeded to take a robust swig and hand the flask back to her. She eyed him with a bit of suspicion. "It'll warm you," he said with a bit of assurance.

Taking his advice, she took a gulp then coughed. With a nod, which he took as her thanks, she offered the flask back to him and continued her wheezing and coughing.

Charlie patted her back and left his hand there until she was breathing again. His thumb smoothed over a patch of bare skin at her neckline until she straightened her back and fixed her eyes on the fire. He pulled back his hand as if he'd just touched a flame. Abruptly, he got up and muttered something about being right back. He went into the woods, cursing himself as he did. When he'd gone far enough that he could no longer see her, he leaned his back against a tree and looked up to the heavens, contemplating how he'd gone daft. He knew why well enough, but no matter how soft and inviting her skin may have felt, it was not his to touch. The poor woman—no matter how appealing—had no interest in or need for anything he had to offer.

Charlie returned, freshly determined to focus on practical matters, only to find she was gone. Fear shot through him as he called out her name.

"Aye?" Her voice came from the darkness a few yards away.

"Where were you?" Without waiting for an answer, he

went toward the sound of her voice until he could make out her form in the darkness. "Come, let's return to the fire." He reached for her hand, missed, and grasped what he hoped was her shoulder. He slid his hand down to her hand, which felt smooth and soft against his.

"Mr. MacDonell?" Mistress Shaw asked after a moment of silence.

He returned to his senses, tightened his grasp on her hand, and led her back to the fire. "Dinnae leave without telling me first," he admonished gruffly. "'Tis not safe to be wandering alone."

"Wandering? 'Tis no business of yours, but I went to the woods to attend to some personal business."

"What if something had happened to you?"

"I suppose I would have screamed, just as I would have if you had known where I was."

Perhaps she had a right to feel as annoyed as she sounded, but he had rights, too. If he was to escort her— for no compensation, no less—she ought not make his job harder. He returned her annoyance with a directness that bordered on harsh. "I'm responsible for you!"

"No one asked you to be!"

"Well, I am whether either of us likes it, and apparently, neither of us does. For the duration of this journey, I'm the best protection you've got against both man and nature, so please do me the courtesy of letting me know where you are at all times!" They stood face-to-face in the darkness. Charlie was fuming, and Mistress Shaw... well, he could only guess at her expression, but he would probably not be far off.

"Very well, then," she said with forced restraint.

Well, that's more like it. He gave himself a smug nod

but then felt her warm breath on his neck and nearly forgot why she annoyed him so.

She went on. "I will do my best to follow your rules, of which—if I might point out—you failed to inform me. Perhaps you could write them all down for me to study tomorrow during the long ride ahead!"

Charlie's jaw dropped. Ah, yes, that was why she annoyed him—and now rendered him speechless. In truth, he had plenty of choice words to say, but he was much too gallant to voice them to a lady. Still, this irritating impudence of hers would have to stop, and there was no better time than the present. He opened his mouth to tell her as much.

"Good night." She turned her back to him, wrapped her cloak tightly about her, and stretched out on the ground on the opposite side of the fire.

Charlie scowled as Mistress Shaw settled down for the night. "Aye, well, we'll talk in the morning."

"Looking forward to it," she said with false—if not defiant—cheer.

Chapter 4

Rules of the Road

The morning's discussion of rules, as she'd called them, was followed by miles of silence, which for the time being was just fine with Charlie. It wasn't until afternoon, when they stopped to water the horse, that Charlie broached the subject he'd been troubling over.

A rushing stream forged a path through thick woods. Mistress Shaw bent down and splashed a handful of cool water on her face then looked up to the sky, while she wiped her face and neck dry with her kertch. Cursed with an appreciation for even the most annoying women, Charlie smiled at how the sun seemed to seek her out through the canopy of tree branches above, lending a bronze sheen to her rich brown hair. She turned toward him. Before her eyes reached his, he averted his gaze and climbed back up the bank. He would be damned if he would let her catch him admiring her. Any other woman might have warmed at the sight, but not this one. Not only did she not deserve any warmth he had to offer, she would no doubt reward him with a sharp look or word.

He was not in the mood. What he needed instead was a dry, mossy spot to lie down for a rest. Once he'd accomplished that, he draped his arm over his eyes and indulged in a moment of peace.

The soft padding of feet signaled her approach, and the quiet rustle of skirts let him know she had sat down beside him. A languid sigh followed, which he could not ignore. Such a sigh could mean so many things. He dared not hope for much, but perhaps a morning's reflection had brought her around. So he opened an eye, just in case, and found her watching the water trip over the rocks. She gave him no apology, not one thought for him. But what had he really expected? Eyes closed once again, he tried to doze.

Moments later, feeling restless, he spoke without bothering to open his eyes. "Mistress Shaw, what would you have done had I not come along?"

"Managed."

"And how, might I ask?"

"Please rest assured I'd not have fared nearly as well without your assistance, and I do thank you for it. Have I not told you as much? If I haven't, forgive me. I am in your debt."

Unsure of her level of sincerity, he opened his eyes to gauge her expression. "That's not what I meant. I only wondered at how you were left so alone. A household that size must require half a dozen house servants, and then there are farm workers. It just seems as though there would have been enough people to come to your aid."

Mistress Shaw looked into his eyes. "I imagine they fled. By the time I made my way outside, they were gone."

She revealed little emotion, but Charlie was vexed.

Her eyes flitted about before settling downward. "My husband knew how to elicit the appearance of respect, but true loyalty was something he must not have inspired, for it surely was absent when needed the most."

Charlie bit off his anger as he thought of the workers leaving her at the mercy of soldiers. His people would have fought to the death for their Glengarry chief and his family as a matter of honor. But her people—or her husband's—had left her to fend for herself. No matter how disagreeable she might have been at times, they owed it to her. Matters of duty and honor came first.

"I promise you this, Mistress Shaw. You will not be abandoned again. I will see you home safely." But even as he said it, Charlie knew he could not guarantee it if anything happened to him.

She lifted her eyes in surprise. "Thank you, Mr. MacDonell." He managed a brief smile before she rose and excused herself to walk away.

He could not help but watch. She had not yet put her hair in her kertch, so thick strands of it, smooth and straight, draped over her shoulders, arriving in a slight inward curve at her waist. For a moment, he wondered how it would feel if he put his hands there. Then he chastised himself. She was grieving and in no need of his touch or any manner of attention he might wish to pay her. He'd spent so much time with women who wanted to please him that he had to remind himself there was the occasional woman who didn't—for example, this woman. She had no desire for anything from him except his protection, which he felt compelled out of honor to provide.

Yes, she needed his help, but to take advantage of this

would be wholly unseemly, even for him. Grieving widow that she was, she would have his respect and his help on her journey. Anything more would be wrong—a phrase he expected to repeat on a regular basis over the following days, while sharing a horse, with her body pressed against his.

They continued their journey on horseback until dusk overtook the long shadows.

"Keep an eye out for a good place to stop for the night," Charlie said.

As they followed a bend in the road, something caught Mistress Shaw's eye. She glanced back once and then again. "Do you see someone back there?"

Charlie turned, scanning the road and the land that lined it. "No."

"I was sure I saw someone," Mistress Shaw insisted.

The next moment, a rider appeared on the road before them, and two riders approached from behind, pistols drawn.

"Highwaymen. Hang on!" He made a sharp turn off the road, urging his horse over the heath as fast as he could safely maneuver. The falling darkness did not make it easy to maneuver over the rough terrain, but it masked their location from their pursuers. If they could make it to the trees up ahead, they might either elude the highwaymen or force them to give up the chase. They were nearly halfway there when they heard the shouts ordering them to stop. A bullet hissed past, far too close.

"Hold tight!" Charlie's horse seemed to fly toward the woods. Making it safely to cover, they wove their way through the trees. Charlie glanced back. "Damn them."

Their pursuers closed in. Moonlight shone through

the branches on the other side of the woods. Beyond the trees, he saw more open space with nowhere to hide. Charlie considered his options. Two people on one horse would be hard-pressed to outrun their pursuers for long, but perhaps they could hide. As hoofbeats approached, Charlie got down from the horse and helped Mistress Shaw to the ground. Even though his warhorse was well-trained, he left him behind just in case he moved or made a sound that might give them away.

He took Mistress Shaw by the hand and led her toward a tree that looked large enough to conceal them. A twig broke close by. Mistress Shaw pressed her back to the tree. Charlie shielded her, pressing his body against hers. The highwayman walked by so closely that Charlie could smell his sweat. When others called out for him, Mistress Shaw's heart pounded against Charlie's chest. She drew in a short breath as she heard some leaves rustle. Charlie covered her mouth with his fingers. The poor woman was shaking with terror. A fierce determination rose within him to protect her. The thought burned with such ferocity, he thought she must feel it, too. Was this how his friend Callum had felt when he'd first met his Mari?

And that was the moment when, aided by the way her body molded to his, the idea of love came to mind. No, he'd gone daft—either that, or the thought of Callum's Mari and the happier times they'd all spent in Edinburgh had planted the idea. Yes, that was all.

Thoughts of love left the next moment as footsteps once more drew near. He leaned closer and pressed his cheek to hers. His lips brushed her ear as he whispered, "Do you trust me?"

Her eyes widened as she shook her head no.

Charlie smiled. "Stay here."

"And just where would I go?" she whispered. Her panic shone through her frustration as he took a step. "Wait! Don't leave me."

He put a finger to his lips and leaned close to murmur into her ear. "Stay still and trust me." He looked into her eyes, and she gave him a terrified nod. He pressed his gunpowder pouch into her hand. "Just in case." The next moment, Charlie leapt up to a branch and swung into the tree. Mistress Shaw loaded her pistol.

Charlie rustled some leaves on his way up and drew the attention of one of the bandits, who then called out. He was striding directly toward Mistress Shaw. She held onto her pistol, now hidden within the folds of her skirt. Now only a few feet away, her attacker glowered at her and reached out.

Charlie swung down from an overhead branch and kicked the bandit in the teeth with a force that sent the man to the ground in a heap. If the sound of their struggle had not alerted the others, the bandit's cry did. The other two thieves were there in an instant. Charlie wielded his sword at one, striking a blow to the highwayman's neck. The force sent him backward as blood soaked through his shirt at the shoulder. He lost consciousness.

A rustling step sounded behind Charlie, but as he turned, sword in hand, ready to swing, he faced the third man, who pointed a pistol squarely at Charlie's chest. In the instant he took to consider his options, a shot rang out, and the man fell to the ground.

Mistress Shaw stepped away from the tree that concealed her. As the smoke rose from her pocket pistol, Charlie peered at her, stunned.

"He was going to kill you."

"Aye, but I didnae expect you to get to him first." He smiled and held out his hand. "Well done, Mistress Shaw." Without hesitation, she grasped his hand as if it were a lifeline, while Charlie whistled for his horse.

He turned to face her, surprised. "Your hand is trembling." His eyes swept up to her full lips and high cheekbones. Soft brown eyes met his.

She spoke in a hush. "I've never killed a man before."

Charlie opened his arms and drew her to him, cradling her head in his hand.

"Will you take me home now?" she whispered.

"Aye, lass." Charlie pulled back, as if he'd awoken from a dream—or a spell. He was the one who was always in charge. He enjoyed being in control of his mind and his senses, both of which he now seemed to be losing. Whatever had prompted this uncomfortable lapse would not overpower him again.

"I'll get one of their horses," she said.

As she started toward the closest one, Charlie grabbed her wrist and stopped her. "'Tis too risky. We're in their territory now. If someone recognizes the horse as belonging to them, there'd be no escaping their wrath."

Conceding his point with a nod, Mistress Shaw turned from the bandit's horse and joined Charlie on his. They made their way out of the woods, and when they reached the clearing, they sped up to a gallop.

IT WAS NOT until hours later that they'd gone far enough for Charlie to feel safe to stop. They made camp for the night, nestled between jutting rocks and a boulder. They could not risk a fire, so there was no cooking or warmth. They supped on the last of the bread and cheese Mistress Shaw had brought from home then slept their usual proper distance apart. This time, it was Charlie who made certain of that.

He did not like the increasing power she held over him, nor did he understand it. He liked women—loved them, in fact. They were one of life's exquisite pleasures. But what he felt for Mistress Shaw was more troubling, or rather, impossible. Of course, that was the appeal. He could not— would not—bed her, which naturally made him want to. That's all that it was—a desire to have what was forbidden. He exhaled in relief. Thank God he had sorted that out.

Then the shuffling sound of her shifting her weight reminded him of how close she was—an arm's length, to be precise.

IN THE MORNING, he returned with some small fish he'd caught in a makeshift net that he'd fashioned from wild oat straw and then left overnight in the stream. Ribbons of sunlight shone down through the trees, illuminating Mistress Shaw. For a moment, he just stood there watching her sleep. Her lips were slightly parted, her chest gently rising and lowering.

Her eyelids fluttered, and she looked up at him. She abruptly sat up and smoothed back her hair. "If you'll excuse me, I'll be back in a moment and ready to leave."

Charlie nodded as he packed up the fish to take with

them for later. While he doubted the highwaymen would continue their chase through the Highlands, he did not want to assume. People died from assumptions like that. So he planned to put more road between them and the bandits before stopping to light a fire and cook the fish he'd just caught.

A cry cut through the mist. Charlie sprang up and ran. "Mistress Shaw?"

"Wait there! Don't come any closer."

Charlie froze, afraid that she might have a dirk to her throat. But she emerged alone with a pained, but dignified, walk and a fierce resolve burning in her eyes. Muscles twitched in her jaw.

"Mistress Shaw?" he cautiously asked.

She shook her head, and his determination weakened to panic.

Charlie thought through all the possible causes for her curious behavior. She had been in the woods, yet not held captive.

"Tell me. What was it? An animal?"

"No."

"Not an animal..." He puzzled it out for himself. If not man or animal, his next guess would be plant. What sort of plant would cause her such distress? He knew of nothing except... "Nettles?" He'd seen some and had intended to mention it to her, but he'd gotten distracted. "Show me your hands."

She held them out, palms up. There were no telltale signs of the rash and red blisters that stinging nettles could cause. "That's not where I... uh... encountered them," she said softly.

Charlie looked toward the place she'd just come from. "No? But you were over there when you cried out."

She let out an exasperated sigh. "Yes, I was over there, but the nettles... I was... well, I was close to the ground."

A moment later, he shut his eyes. "Oh, lassie." It took little thought to imagine her squatting down to relieve herself, only to discover a patch of nettles beneath her. Had it been one of his friends or fellow soldiers, he would have laughed, but he couldn't laugh at her. She was so proper and horrified by it all that Charlie felt truly sorry for her and for the resulting misery that would soon drive her to distraction. He had come across stinging nettles before and suffered the rash the poisonous plant could inflict, but he'd never been afflicted in so sensitive a place.

She nodded, confirming his inevitable conclusion. Then she looked away, but her narrowing eyes could not hide the pain. Her mood worsened as she shifted her weight from one foot to the other, and tears welled up in her eyes. "Oh, it itches unbearably!"

He took hold of her hand and began long strides toward the woods, but she pulled back. "No! Please, stop! It hurts too much!"

With barely a moment's thought, he scooped her up into his arms, carried her to the edge of a stream, and set her back on her feet. "Take your clothes off and sit down in the water."

She looked at him as though he were mad, but his stern look forced her silence. "It's either that or wear wet clothing that willnae dry in this damp air and then sleep on the cool ground in wet clothes. I'll not let you fall ill."

In too much discomfort to argue, she gave him a pathetically miserable look. "May I leave my shift on?"

Since he had met her, she'd maintained a certain grace in spite of her tragic and sometimes undignified circumstances. She had a heart strong as any man he'd known—stronger than many. To see her undone by a plant sent a pang of pity through him.

He fought back a warm smile, but his mouth turned up at one corner. "Here, keep your shift dry, and wear this." With no warning, he slipped his léine out from under his plaid and pulled it off over his head. His action drew a slight gasp of shock from Mistress Shaw as she spied his bare chest. But Charlie noted that she did not turn entirely away. Suppressing a grin, he placed the léine in her hand. "Go on. Put it on. I'll not look."

True to his word, he turned and kept his back to her while he put his jacket back on over his shirtless torso. When he could hear no movement from her, he asked, "Are you dressed?"

"Not properly so, but I suppose you could call it that."

He turned to find her looking far better in his léine than he ever had. He led her to the stream, which was small and shallow, and they walked along the edge until they found an ankle-deep pool she could sit in. He could not imagine how she kept from dissolving into tears. Still, her agonizing discomfort could not be concealed.

Charlie was tender and kind as he spoke to her. "Get every... uh... part wet that was touched by the nettles. The cool water will help ease the itching."

She winced at the mere suggestion of the rash's location on her person, but the walls of propriety had already been breached. Pain had a way of bypassing formalities. She carefully shifted her position and eased herself further into the water, but her hand slipped on a rock, and she fell backward.

"I've got you." He caught her and held her for what he began to sense was too long, but she was too good a fit in his arms. Charlie moved his hands to her shoulders and gave them a squeeze as he stood. "I'll go tend to the horse. While I'm gone, try and wash off what's left of the nettles."

She glanced up, but stopped short of meeting his eyes. She took in a breath as though she might speak but gave up with a nod.

MISTRESS SHAW SPENT the morning riding behind Charlie in silent misery. Only an occasional intake of air and a tightening grip about his waist gave away her discomfort. Never once did she complain. In truth, Charlie wouldn't have blamed her, but she suffered in silence. He admired her for it. In the late afternoon, he stopped near a stream that flowed down from a hill. Mistress Shaw spoke little, except to excuse herself and head toward the cool water in haste. When she returned some time later, properly dressed, her face showed less strain.

Charlie was crouched down before a fire when he heard her approach, and looked up. "We'll have grouse for supper." A winning smile bloomed on his face.

She responded in kind, although her smile held a weary warmth. "Mr. MacDonell, I don't know how to thank you."

He suppressed his surprise at her improved demeanor. "'Tis just a bird."

"Not the supper, though I thank you for that, too."

He looked up. "You're quite welcome, Mistress Shaw." He returned to his cooking, only partially hiding his pleasure, while Mistress Shaw hung his léine over a branch to dry. But his thoughts remained on the woman now seated beside him.

THE NEXT DAY, they rode in amiable silence, speaking of practical matters when needed. The sun had dipped down behind the heather-hued hills ahead, when Charlie found himself enjoying the warmth of Mistress Shaw's body against his. She had dozed off, and her head lay on the back of his shoulder. Her clasped hands slipped apart, and she slid to the right. Charlie reached a sturdy arm back just in time to keep her from falling.

With a start, she awoke and grabbed his arm, righting herself.

"'Tis all right." Charlie looked ahead for a suitable place to stop so she could rest.

She sighed. "I'm sorry."

"Whatever for?"

"I ken that I'm slowing you down, as it is. You shouldnae have to hold onto me, too."

Charlie nearly said that he never minded holding onto a braw lassie, but he clamped his mouth shut. Had he become so used to charming pretty women that such words came without thought? He would have to do better, for she was not the sort to appreciate idle flattery. That thought alone made him pause to consider her effect upon him. Who was she to him that he should worry about what to say? He'd never thought about words. He'd just said what he wanted to say—or what women wanted to hear. Either way, they never seemed to object. He understood women, and they liked him—well, most women—except Isobel Shaw. He had a feeling she tolerated him, solely because she had little choice if she hoped to get home. Or perhaps she did not entirely mind him. He couldn't tell. And that was what most irked him about her. He was never quite sure where he stood. He'd never put a good deal of thought into whether—or why—women liked him. They just did—not all, but enough. And he'd always been able to tell the difference with ease. Those who were willing, he loved in return. Those who weren't? Well, he was usually too busy with the former to think any more of the latter. So why was this woman plaguing his thoughts?

Charlie frowned and gave his head a shake. "By the Rood, I've gone daft," he muttered.

"Because you're helping me?"

"Sorry?" It took him a moment to retrace his thoughts, which he seemed to have spoken aloud.

She looked down and nodded. "You just said you've gone daft."

He glanced back over his shoulder. "Oh, that. I've gone daft on my own. I didnae need your assistance for that." He laughed it off, but her silence, and the fact that he couldn't turn around to read her expression, troubled him to no end.

"Mr. MacDonell, you've been more than kind, but you've no obligation to me, I assure you."

"When I spoke, I was thinking of something else, not you. No, I feel no obligation to you, which is not to say that I'd leave you." *God's wounds, man!* He went on, though his gut told him to stop. "You would give me great pleasure—that is, *it* would give me great pleasure—to bring you home, to your home, of course. I assure you, I feel no obligation. On the contrary, I want you... *to*... I want *to*..." *Good God, man, stop talking.* "I want *to* see you home safely."

"When do you think that will be?"

Charlie exhaled and refocused his thoughts. "It depends. We're about two days from my home. I'd like to stop there for a night or two, if I may, for I've not seen my family in years. Would you mind very much?"

"Of course not, but you're kind to ask."

Charlie looked back over his shoulder with a crooked grin. "Kind? Now, Mistress Shaw, mustn't jump to conclusions."

Chapter 5

The Crossroads

They arrived at a crossroads at the foot of a loch in the glen, where a thatch-roofed inn stood, looking warm and inviting. They left the horse with a stableboy, who said there were vacant rooms. As it turned out, there was one.

Before Isobel could protest, Charlie said they would take it. He cast her a sideways look that ensured her silence, but she was not happy about it. Without even a glance, he took a firm grip on her hand and led her up to the room. Once inside, Charlie set down his saddlebag, while Isobel glanced about at the dark, smoke-stained rafters, stone walls, a coarse, linen-clad bed, and a table.

Charlie sighed. "Warm, dry shelter, at last."

"Mr. MacDonell, this is in no way proper."

"Nor was traveling together and sleeping as close as we'll be in this room, but we've done it, and we'll continue to do so."

"But folks will think—"

"That we're married."

She gasped. "Which we're not!"

"Then we'll tell them we're not."

"But that's worse!"

Charlie shrugged. "Let them think what they want. No one here kens nor cares who you are."

Isobel strode over and planted herself before him. "I do, and sharing a room is out of the question."

"It isn't a question."

Much to her consternation, Charlie laughed.

"Mr. MacDonell—"

"I'll not touch you, if that's what you're thinking. Look, dearie, all I want is a few swigs of ale, a hot meal, and some rest. Unless you're one of those three, I assure you, you're safe from me."

Isobel found his casual disregard for her reputation and feelings intolerable, and she took in a breath to tell him as much.

Charlie smiled and interrupted her before she could begin. "You've made it this far unscathed. Can you not manage to grant me a wee bit of trust?"

She considered his words as her eyes wandered to the bed. It was cleaner than most and looked soft and inviting. Her rash from the nettles was not quite fully healed. Refusing this room would mean one more night outside on the cold, hard ground. She lifted her eyes. "You'll sleep on the floor?"

Charlie's eyes lit with mischief. "If I must."

It annoyed her to no end that he found this amusing. "Oh, aye, you most certainly must!"

He chuckled. "Calm yourself, dearie. I'll sleep on the floor."

"Where on the floor?"

"By the door, far away from the bed."

"Very well," she said with a nod.

"Good. Now then, Mistress Shaw, shall we go down to supper?" Charlie offered his arm with mock formality and a hint of a smirk. It did not escape her notice, but she chose to ignore it. Instead, she took his arm and descended the stairs to the tavern.

Evening had fallen, and the light from the windows had faded. In its place, warm pools of lamplight and a dwindling fire in the large stone fireplace cast soft light on the smoke-stained walls and dark beams overhead. The place smelled of smoking embers, ale, and wool, dampened by the bodies of road-weary travelers—a dozen of whom were scattered about the small room. The innkeeper, a young widow, held onto two flagons of ale as she smiled warmly at Charlie. He met her lingering gaze with a grin. She leaned closer and whispered something to him. He glanced over at Mistress Shaw then grinned at the widow. Isobel bristled as the woman looked her up and down before she turned back and said something to Charlie. He let out a deep laugh, leaned closer, and spoke through his grin. Then he took the ale and returned to the table.

"Enjoying yourself?" Isobel cringed to hear how she sounded—like a jealous wife, which was a ridiculous notion. How did he manage to bring out the worst in her?

Charlie could do what he liked. He was nothing to her. She was the one who kept her head level in any situation. Calm people who maintained control made the best decisions—and protected their hearts.

Why would that come to mind? Isobel dismissed the thought. One heartbreak had been more than enough. She was young and fell prey to a handsome young man's flattering words and professions of love. The worst part was that he'd never cared for her, let alone deserved her. Years later, she still remembered the pain—not of the heartache, but of realizing how stupid she'd been.

He had swaggered about the lists, all broad shoulders and muscles, stealing glances at her. When he'd found her alone one day, gathering herbs, he'd taken her basket and carried it for her. That was all it took for him to capture her heart—that and a pair of gray eyes. With those soft eyes, he had taken her into his soul, or so she had thought. He was artful and false, and he kissed her and made her feel loved. It was thrilling—until she couldn't breathe. It happened too fast for her heart to absorb it. When she asked him to stop, he did. Then he grinned and coaxed her. She was young and naive. After he'd tried long enough to persuade her to lie in the tall grass with him, his face changed. "I'll not ask you again," he said.

And he hadn't.

Never again would she allow her heart to rule her head. She knew now that it hadn't been love, but she'd felt it as deeply. It was the stuff that broke lassies' hearts. Perhaps that was worse than true love, for one never forgot self-loathing.

It never happened again. No man was allowed close enough. From that point on, Isobel made sensible choices. She married a sensible man with position and holdings enough to provide her with a sensible life for the rest of her days—or until something senseless would happen. Even that had worked to her advantage. She had not wanted love, for love was too unpredictable. So when her husband had died, she felt the grief anyone felt when a man lost his life—no more and no less. She had suffered the tragic loss of her husband and felt sorrow for him, but no heartache.

Yet here she was now, full of a burning vexation that didn't become a young widow at all—and all because Charlie MacDonell, with his daring blue eyes and his confident grin, made her feel when she ought to be thinking. Where was her strong will when she needed it most?

Charlie was looking at her with a concern she could not believe was sincere. "Are you all right?"

"I'm fine, thank you." She wasn't.

The widowed innkeeper delivered a bowl of stew to each of them, but Charlie's came with an inviting smile. No words were exchanged, but the looks between the woman and Charlie were enough to prompt Isobel to roll her eyes and direct her attention to her meal.

Charlie grinned as he watched the widow return to her duties. He then made several attempts to begin a conversation with Isobel, each of which she cut short with one or two words. She couldn't help herself. In this strange place, she felt ill at ease. Charlie, on the other hand, had a way of turning strangers into friends within minutes of meeting. How could a man like that feel genuine interest in anybody? She was sure he could not. He was just another man using his looks, which she couldn't deny were impressive, as well as his charm— devastating, if she had to be honest—to get what he wanted. All of these attributes led to a question that dominated her thoughts for the rest of the meal. What did he want from her?

With the question left unresolved, they went up to their room for the night. Isobel kept reminding herself that they were no closer together now than when they'd slept outside. But a closed room was different.

With barely a word, Charlie settled down for the night on the floor by the door. He was true to his word. She could not fault him for that. In fact, since she had met him, he had been nothing short of a gentleman toward her. So what troubled her now? Was it the broad smile he'd flashed at the innkeeper? The image lingered in her mind. How might it feel to be looked at like that?

She had to ignore that thought, for it was the sort of thought that could burn in one's heart if one let it, which she would not. No, she had learned to ignore such emotions. But the more she tried to dismiss the man lying not all that far away, the louder his every move seemed as he settled to sleep. She could not help but wonder about him down there, all alone on the floor, while she lay in her bed... all alone.

A ROOSTER ANNOUNCED A NEW DAY. For a brief moment before she opened her eyes, Isobel thought she was home. But the feel of the coarsely woven bedding against her skin brought her back to the inn. The room was still dark, so she got up and opened the shutters. Sun was just beginning to lighten the misty gray morning outside.

"We might get some rain today," Isobel said before turning to discover that Charlie was gone. She glanced about the small room as if she might find him in a corner. But Charlie MacDonell was gone, along with his saddlebags.

Having no baggage of her own, Isobel needed only to wrap her airisaid about her. The next moment, she was on her way down the stairs and out the front door. She walked past the innkeeper with barely a nod as she strode to the stable. To her surprise, Charlie's horse was still there, as was Charlie, asleep on the hay. Having formed her own conclusion of what had transpired, Isobel nudged Charlie's shoulder with the tip of her shoe, a bit more firmly than necessary. "Shall we go?" Without waiting for a response, she started to lift up the saddle, but Charlie sprang up and took over the job.

Charlie looked at her with a puzzled expression. "I thought we might enjoy a hearty breakfast first."

"Well, from the looks of it, you've already enjoyed what this inn has to offer," she said brusquely.

Taken aback, Charlie studied her. "Aye? Well, whatever it is that has ruffled your feathers, we'll have a long day on the road to discuss it. But right now, there's a fine Scottish breakfast inside, and I'm going to have it—with or without you, Mistress Crabbit."

Isobel opened her mouth to protest but was speechless. Mistress Crabbit, indeed! If she was a bit grouchy, she had good enough reason... except that she didn't. So what if he had left the room and gone downstairs to find that pretty innkeeper? Was that any business of hers? He had every right to do what he pleased, regardless of whether she agreed with his choices. He owed nothing to her. And the truth was, she owed everything to him. She was behaving like a foolish young girl who had no understanding of the ways of the world. That was not who she was, or at least it was not who she had chosen to be. She was a calm and sensible woman, or she had been until she met Charlie MacDonell.

She paused at the threshold of the inn then quietly opened the door. There he was, at a dark wooden table, enjoying his meal. He glanced up and saw her but returned his attention to the food on the table. Isobel sat down to join him. The innkeeper appeared out of nowhere and asked Isobel if she cared for something to eat.

Isobel nodded. "Yes, please." When the woman had gone, Isobel stared at her hands and exhaled. "I'm sorry."

Charlie glanced at her, nodded, and continued to eat.

Isobel cleared her throat and continued. "I woke up and saw you were gone, and it scared me. I thought you might have left me." She inwardly cringed, for although the thought had crossed her mind briefly, it had not been her first thought. The look on his face the next moment, when his eyes met hers, confirmed that he knew it as well.

Isobel's gaze flitted about the room before settling upon her folded hands and the table they rested upon. Soon, her plate was delivered. Eating gave her something to do to distract from the gnawing uneasiness churning within her. They passed the remainder of their meal in silence.

Charlie finished eating first and went to the bar for another flagon of ale. He stayed there while Isobel finished her meal alone. Before leaving, Charlie thanked the innkeeper for her fine cooking and ale.

"Come back soon," the woman said, her eyes smiling.

Charlie winked. "I'd love to, dearie."

A woman could spend days thinking back on that smile. Why hadn't Isobel noticed it before? Had he not smiled at her? What business did she have even noticing smiles? But she had. Well, that needed to stop. *You're a fool, Isobel Shaw.*

ALL MORNING, they rode through a thick mist that clung to the ground. It took most of the morning to work their way up a steep, rocky hill laced with rivulets of water that made the ground slick underfoot. Riding was out of the question, given the steep incline, so Charlie led his horse, while Mistress Shaw walked beside him until they arrived at the crest of the brae. There they stopped, breathing deeply.

"You wouldnae ken in this fog, but there's a bonnie glen down there somewhere." Unexpected longing gripped Charlie's chest as he thought of how close home was. "'Tis not safe to go further, so I'll build a fire to chase away the damp while we wait here for it to clear."

The sights he'd imagined so many times lay before him, almost within reach, but he could not see them. Still, he would soon walk through the door to his croft and greet his mother, the only family he had left. His brother, Hugh, had died during the killing times in Edinburgh. The familiar guilt gripped him, as it always did when he thought about Hugh. Something inside Charlie had broken when he lost Hugh. It was clearer now more than ever that he was not the same man he had been when he'd crossed over this land five years ago. Hugh was gone, as were more friends than he could bear to count. Each loss took a part of his soul.

He'd managed to fill up the void by signing on with

any army willing to pay. And then there were the women. He loved all of them while he was with them and remembered some of them when he was not. But in time, not even they were enough to fill the empty places in his heart. So he followed his heart's calling and set out for his home in the Highlands.

A gentle breeze brushed Mistress Shaw's hair against his arm, reminding him she was there. He found her quiet presence a comfort, although he could not say why. She shivered and took in a sharp breath.

"Are you cold, Mistress Shaw?"

Before she could answer, he pulled part of his plaid loose and wrapped it over her shoulders. There he held it in place, and they breathed in the smell of rain-soaked grass and wet earth.

"I'm sorry I frightened you this morning."

Her cheeks flushed as she shook her head. "Oh, that! It was nothing. I dinnae ken why I made such a fuss."

He gazed into her eyes, and they softened. "You've had quite a difficult week." As he looked into her eyes, Charlie was seized with an uncharacteristic shyness. "And of course, traveling with me cannae be easy." He started to offer the same winning grin that had served him so well, but he found himself wanting to shed it in favor of honesty. "I didnae spend the night with the innkeeper."

She took in a breath but said nothing at first. Then she looked away. "Mr. MacDonell, 'tis no business of mine how you spend your nights," she said softly.

Charlie had seen her look uncomfortable before, but never like this. "I've upset you again."

"No, I'm not upset! I just dinnae ken what to say. I

can understand how my behavior this morning might have led you to believe I expected an explanation. But of course, you don't owe me any. I was behaving like... I dinnae ken. I woke up. You were gone. I was still half asleep. And I thought... It was none of my business."

"You were right." He looked frankly at her, but she averted her eyes before he could read her expression. It was something he'd almost always been able to do with women, but with Mistress Shaw, he was never quite sure what she was thinking. Just as he was accepting defeat, her lips spread slightly, suggesting a smile. It moved him to go on with the rest of the truth. "Sally—that was her name—asked me to meet her last night, and I did."

Mistress Shaw's back straightened. "Please, I don't need to hear more."

Charlie stood to face her, but she turned her back to him. Undeterred, he went on. "I told her thank you, but I declined her proposal. It occurred to me that had I returned to our room in the dark, there's a good chance you'd have shot me. I didnae ken where that pistol of yours was." He grinned, but turned around as she was, it was wasted on her. His smile faded. With a gentle hand on her shoulder, he turned her to face him and looked into her eyes. "I didnae want to be with her."

The words she might have said next were left spoken, but she lifted her eyes to meet his. As they stood at the top of the brae, the mist lifted, unnoticed.

"Mistress Shaw?"

Her lips parted to answer, but no words came. She turned away.

"Isobel?"

Her gaze drifted reluctantly back, and as her soft brown eyes met his, he gave in to his impulse to kiss her— a warm and lingering kiss that was lovely and wrong. And the longer it lasted, the surer he was that it was wrong. But he did not stop. He gave in to desire as he usually did, because he usually could. Only this time, he thought of the consequences.

Wisps of green land and gray rocks jutted out through the gray mist below. Isobel gently took a step backward, shaking her head. "Charlie."

He searched her eyes. "What?"

"I just wanted to say it."

"My name?"

"Aye."

He was transfixed. "If you say it again, I will kiss you again."

She smiled warmly. "No, I won't, nor will you."

But he wanted her to. He wanted to hear his name from her lips and her soft intake of breath when he leaned down to kiss her.

"I'm a widow, behaving like a foolish young girl. And you—"

"I'm a rogue?"

Her smile was soft and forgiving. "Oh, aye, that you are."

"And a cotter's son?"

Her face flushed as she lowered her eyes to avoid his fiery gaze. "You're a man I should never have kissed."

His eyes darkened, and his voice had an edge. "But *I* kissed *you*, so your conscience is clear."

She flashed a protesting look but said nothing. And

then Charlie knew the connection between them could not be denied. Nor did he want to deny it, and the startling truth of that struck him. For some time, he had sensed it there, lingering, patiently waiting just under the surface. Everything had been wrong—their circumstances, their timing, their stations in life—things that Charlie had known all along. Yet in the face of it all, the pull of their hearts had grown stronger until it had become first unbearable, and then undeniable.

With each glimpse beyond her well-practiced facade, he saw more feeling and passion. It reflected his own. He'd known it as surely as if she had told him in words how she felt. Even now, if he pressed her, he doubted she would deny it. How could she after that kiss? All they could deny now was having a future together, and that, she would most certainly do. Whatever they had or could be to each other was over before it had started, for Isobel had made a decision. And whatever that kiss was, it had nothing to do with their lives from this point forward.

Isobel went to the horse and made a show of arranging her things. Charlie knew she was hiding her feelings, but she could not hide the feel of her lips touching his. He still felt it. He wanted to go to her and confront her, to grab hold of her shoulders and force her to look into his eyes and admit that she felt something for him. And he could have. But it would have driven her further away.

If he'd learned anything about women over the years, it was that trying to force things only drove them further away. He had never forced his presence on a woman, nor would he now. If she wanted her precious solitude, she would have it. He would, however, live up to his promise to see her home safely. After that, her life would be her own—without him. She could sit in her home, safely alone, and pretend their kiss hadn't happened.

But Charlie would never forget it.

Chapter 6

Coming Home

The morning rain had eased to a drizzle as they rode along the dirt path that led to Invergarry. Ahead, a small group of thatched cottages stood huddled together in the shadow of the castle. There was no one about fetching milk or dry wood from the cow shed. All was still except for the sound of soft rain and horse hooves stepping on wet stones and dirt.

Drenched and chilled by the rain, Isobel clung to Charlie as they rode down the path. Thin plumes of smoke rose from the crofts and released the faint scent of peat fire, which wafted through the damp air. Isobel longed for a chair by one of those fires. When Charlie's back stiffened, Isobel lifted her head to see what the cause might be. Charlie turned enough to reveal his clenched jaw. Although a small thing, it was the first glimpse of unbidden emotion he'd revealed since they met. Charlie turned off the path and rode around to the back of a croft, where a small byre shared a wall with the house. Isobel exhaled in relief that the livestock were not kept inside, as was often the custom, then she felt guilty for it. Expressing such feelings would put distance between Charlie and her, which was the last thing she wanted. The realization of this made her pause. What was she thinking to allow feelings like this? She wasn't. She'd stopped thinking because she liked feeling.

From some deeply ingrained force of habit, her good sense emerged, reminding her that she was recently widowed. She had married a stranger. Of course, that was no excuse. She gave her head a slight shake. She'd learned more about her husband after his death than she'd known during his life. How could that be? In some ways, she felt she knew Charlie better than she'd known her own husband.

They dismounted and tethered the horse in a dry corner of the byre. Charlie froze for a moment.

"Is something the matter?"

He forced a smile. "No. I—just a chill. Someone walked over my grave." He shrugged it off. With a smile, he took Isobel's hand and led her to the front door. Letting go of her hand, he gave the door a firm rap.

She missed the strength and warmth of his hand.

The door swung open, and a young woman answered. Wild, deep red waves framed her face, having escaped the loose tie confining the rest of her shoulder-length hair. A moment of shock was soon followed by delight, and she threw her arms about Charlie's neck.

"Charlie! You're home!" She leaned back long enough to put her hands on his face then pressed herself to him again.

Charlie put his hands on her waist and leaned back with a grin. "Bessie MacRanie."

The smile they shared gave rise to suspicions that Isobel found difficult to deny. They'd been lovers. Nothing she observed clouded that image. It forced her to look away, and the fire drew her gaze. As they all went inside, Isobel must have moved toward it, for Bessie MacRanie looked at her then at Charlie.

"Who's your friend?"

The extent of Charlie's surprise at being brought to his senses did not sit well with Isobel. Her look would have told him as much had he bothered to do more than glance in her direction.

"Oh, I'm sorry! How could I forget?"

Isobel raised an eyebrow.

He went on. "Bessie MacRanie—"

"Bess," the woman said with a nod and a smile.

As if unaware, Charlie continued. "This is Isobel Shaw."

"Shaw?" She let out a laugh upon hearing the surname. "I thought you might have brought home a wife."

"A wife? Bessie." While Charlie did not join her in laughing, his enthusiastic denial made Isobel feel a bit slighted.

Bess hooked her arm into Charlie's and led him to the fire. "Come and sit down." She glanced back over her shoulder as if Isobel were an afterthought. "Come along, Mistress Shaw."

"'Tis a bit warm in here already," Isobel muttered.

Bess was halfway to the fireplace when Charlie spoke. "First, I'd like to see my ma."

Bess stopped and turned to him, her face ashen. "Your ma? Charlie, did you not hear?"

Charlie's face lost all expression.

"She's gone," Bess said plainly.

For a long moment, he was still. Bess hooked her arm back into his. "Come sit down."

"When?"

"Months ago."

"How many?"

"Oh, Charlie, 'tis been five months—no, six."

Charlie spoke more to himself than anyone else. "Six months."

"Aye. The laird said I could live here until you came back as long as my brother helped work the land." She lowered her voice. "Och, in truth, since he got married, it's been too small a place for the three of us. Why he married her, I'll never understand. Och, but I'm sorry. You dinnae care to hear about that." She gave his arm a small tug. "Sit down, Charlie. I'll make you some tea—or perhaps something stronger?" When he did not respond, she nodded. "Something stronger."

Isobel sat down in the only other chair nearby and reached out to touch Charlie's folded hands. "I'm so sorry."

He lifted his head to acknowledge her words but not enough to meet her sympathetic gaze. His brow creased as he leaned on his elbows and stared at his hands.

Bess arrived with three cups. As she handed the first to Isobel, she managed to splash a bit over the side of the cup onto Isobel's skirt. With a hasty apology, she scooted a stool over and sat down between them. He reflexively took the whisky glass offered and drank while she put a comforting hand on his shoulder.

Isobel sat back in her chair and watched Bess lean

closer, until her shoulder touched Charlie's. As she spoke, she tucked her hand into the crook of his arm and stroked his forearm with the other. "When it grew too much for her to manage, I came by every day to clean and cook for her. I didnae mind at all. I was happy to help her—and happy to not have to eat Lucy's cooking. No, really, it's terrible! Anyway, your ma was waiting for you to come home."

Charlie lifted his eyes to meet Bess's.

She nodded, affirming, and smiled. Her eyes shone with assurance and a warmth that made Isobel cringe.

"Aye," Bess said softly. "'I want to see Charlie,' she'd say."

"Did she say anything else before..."

Bess shook her head and looked down. "I swept—" Her voice broke. "I swept up the cottage and tucked in her quilt to make sure she was warm, then I went home for the evening. When I came back in the morning, she was gone." Bess laid her head on Charlie's shoulder while he stared down at his hands.

The only sign of emotion was a tear that clung to his lashes and the choked sound of his voice as he thanked her. He abruptly got up and walked outside.

Isobel watched the door close. "I imagine he's gone to her grave."

"Aye." Bess was studying her. Feeling awkward, Isobel averted her gaze to the fire.

"Have you known Charlie long?"

Isobel looked back to the source of her discomfort. "No, just a few days—a week, perhaps."

Bess nodded. "A week, is it?"

Something in her tone grated Isobel. "Aye."

"And he brought you home, did he?" Her words were innocent enough, but her meaning was not.

"Well, no, not in that way."

"No?"

"No. We're just passing through."

"Passing through?"

"Aye, on the way to my home."

Bess lifted an eyebrow. "Oh, to your home?"

Isobel took a deep breath and exhaled. "Miss—"

"Bess."

Isobel nodded. "Bess. Charlie found me..." She paused, seeing Bess's eyes widen, but she chose to ignore it and proceed. "I was stranded through no fault of my own." She was not about to recount the painful details for this woman, who did not deserve them. "Charlie was gallant enough to escort me safely home, for which I'm deeply grateful. That is all. Now, if you'll excuse me, I'm in need of some air." She rose and, as graciously as she could manage, left. She spotted a church steeple jutting above the thatched rooftops and followed it until she saw the churchyard ahead. There, she found Charlie on his knees in front of his mother's gravestone. Despite Isobel's quiet approach, he must have heard her. "Leave me," he said firmly.

"Charlie, I'm sorry."

He forced a nod. "Thank you. But I need some time here."

She wanted to offer him comforting words, but what words could do that? As she'd only minutes ago been made clearly aware, she barely knew him. Yes, they had shared a kiss, but a kiss could mean everything or nothing. After all, she'd met him while he was fleeing someone. It took little imagination to guess that he'd been up to some mischief. He was no thief. She knew him well enough to feel certain of that. He was honest, kind, and chivalrous enough to come to her aid. But he was too charming by half. A kiss meant little, if anything, to a man like Charlie MacDonell. And now he had asked her to leave, so she did.

With no place else to go, she went back to the cottage. Had there been anywhere else to seek refuge, she would have. Instead, she was back at Bess's door. Rather than continue along the previous conversational lines, Isobel chose to take charge. "How long have you known Charlie?"

"My whole life."

"So you've always lived—"

"In the next cottage, aye. We played together as children. Charlie was older, of course." She touched her skin, which Isobel could not deny, was quite lovely—luminous like fine china. She was younger than Isobel, one and twenty, at the most. But her hands were the hands of a farm girl, rough and callused. Isobel took a breath and inwardly chastised herself for being petty. The poor girl had done little to merit her judgment. Of course she and Charlie would be close friends. They'd grown up together. Kind as he was, Charlie would have looked out for her as a brother might do.

Bess poured more whisky into their cups. "He was my first kiss."

The light in her eyes made Isobel wonder if there might have been more than a kiss.

Bess gave a nod. "Oh, I'd loved him for years. All the girls did! Still do. How could you not?"

How could you not? Isobel tried not to roll her eyes.

"And he loved them, too. Charlie had a way." She gave Isobel a conspiratorial look. "Still does. But of course, you ken that. Nae doubt he's won your heart, too."

Her words caught Isobel off guard. She felt color rush to her cheeks. The image of Charlie's kiss was vivid in her mind, but she did her best to replace it with indignant shock. Some truth must have shone through, for Bess's face bloomed to a broad grin. "Oh, dinnae fash. 'Tis not your fault—nor his, really. With such braw looks and that manly way of his, how could anyone resist? And why would they?" Bess leaned her head back as she sighed. "Oh, that Charlie. How many hearts—and bodies—must he have thrilled?"

Isobel flashed an icy look. "I'm afraid you're mistaken."

Bess nodded slowly, not quite hiding a skeptical smile.

Isobel straightened her posture and lifted her chin. "I've just lost my husband, so I'll thank you to keep your untoward imaginings to yourself!"

"I'm so sorry. I didnae ken. Charlie neglected to mention—"

"And what did Charlie neglect to mention?" Charlie closed the door and went straight to the whisky. He filled the cup he'd left sitting on the table then sank into his chair.

Bess glided over to Charlie and stood behind his chair, resting her hands on his shoulders. "I didnae ken that Mistress Shaw was a widow in mourning."

Charlie's eyes darted to Isobel's and softened. "She's not had an easy time, which is why I offered to escort her home to her family."

The mention of family drew an unexpected surge of emotion, which Isobel worked to tamp down.

The strain of the moment was not lost on Charlie, who had not yet taken his eyes from her. With the news of his mother's passing, they both knew grief too well. "We'll have you home soon, Mistress Shaw. I promise." He offered a kind look that warmed Isobel's heart.

But Bess's words and sly looks lingered, taunting her. She wondered if she weren't yearning too much for the warmth of Charlie's gaze. Was it all just his rakish charm, which she now understood was abundantly given? Had she merely taken her place at the end of a long line of ladies? She closed her eyes for a moment.

"We've had quite a long journey." Charlie stood and took his empty cup to the wash basin. "I'd planned to stay here in my mother's home, but now we find ourselves with no place to stay for the night."

"But of course you'll stay here! You're to stay here as long as you like."

Isobel watched the exchange, sure that Bess meant every word, and then some, where Charlie was concerned. That was when she began to do some quick mathematics. Three people and two box beds would make for an awkward arrangement—for Isobel, at least. She had no doubt that Bess would feel no such discomfort.

Charlie interrupted the awkward silence. "I'll sleep on the floor by the fireplace, of course."

Bess shot a look to Charlie but held back whatever it was she looked eager to say.

No longer willing to wait for her hostess to offer, Isobel asked, "And where shall I sleep?"

Torn from her thoughts, Bess turned to Isobel and tilted her head toward a bed in the corner. "Over there."

Charlie seemed unaware of any tension between the two women. "That was the bed Hugh and I shared as boys."

Bess's eyes lit with recollection. "Oh, dear Hughie."

"He grew into quite a man. You should have seen him in Edinburgh, stealing women from me!" Charlie grinned, but sadness soon crept into his expression.

Bess laughed. "Well, he always had your eyes, and as he grew older, there was something in his mouth when he'd say certain things—a wee bit of a grin that reminded me of you." Her eyes softened and settled on Charlie's lips for a moment, then she lifted her eyes to meet his. "Those were happy times here, were they not?"

The warm smile he offered would have made any woman's face light up. Bess glowed as she basked in Charlie's gaze—so much so that Isobel felt like an intruder.

"Ah, well." Charlie turned to Isobel. "You must be tired."

She was, but the hint came so abruptly, it felt like a stab. "Oh, aye, 'tis time for some sleep. Thank you, Bess. Goodnight, Mr. MacDonell." Barely glancing at him, she turned. She climbed into the box bed and pulled the curtains closed. She undressed awkwardly in the small space and reminded herself of her own words to Bess. She was a widow in mourning. Her husband may have been a near stranger, but that did not make her current feelings any more proper. She loathed herself for it. As she settled in under the covers, she could not help but overhear—as she was no doubt meant to.

"'Tis so cold on the floor." Bess's lilting voice rang out like a clear bell.

Charlie chuckled. "I've the embers to warm me."

"Aye, so you do. I suppose that's enough."

Isobel was certain that Bess would delight in warming whatever the embers couldn't reach. With that thought, she yanked the quilt—Charlie's quilt—over her shoulders and ears.

After a soft clinking of cups being put by the basin, Bess spoke again. "I've had quite a long day myself." She lowered her voice. "Make yourselves at home, Charlie. If there's anything you need—anything at all—help yourself."

"Thank you. I'm sure I'll be fine."

Tormented by the quiet that followed, Isobel stole a glance through a small gap in the bed curtains—a mistake, as it turned out, for she spied Bess throwing her arms about Charlie and combing her fingers through his sand-colored hair. Isobel had felt that same hair brush her face as she'd ridden behind him. She rolled her eyes at her own foolishness then closed them.

"Goodnight, Bessie." He put his hands on her wrists for a moment then gently removed them from around his neck.

Bessie shrugged and gave her head a slight shake. "'Tis a cold bed you've chosen, but suit yourself. Good night, Charlie."

Isobel rolled over and stared at the stone wall, which, at the moment, was the only thing in the cottage that didn't vex her.

Chapter 7

Solitude

A firm rap on the thick cottage door brought Charlie to his feet, sword in hand.

"Put your sword down, 'tis I," Callum, tall and sturdy as ever, called in through the window.

With a laugh, Charlie strode over and threw open the door. There stood Callum with his wife, Mari. "Good Lord, look at you, woman!" He opened his arms and embraced a very pregnant Mari then gave Callum a hearty embrace.

"Careful, you'll crush the bannocks!" Mari took the basket from Callum's arm and handed it over to Bess. Isobel emerged from behind the bed curtains, brushing wisps of brown hair into place and pulling a shawl about her shoulders. Mari offered a warm but curious smile. "Charlie, will you nae introduce us?"

"Aye, Mari, I was getting to that. Allow me to introduce Mistress Isobel Shaw. When I made her acquaintance, she was in need of an escort. As her home is not far from here, I was happy to assist her on her journey."

Mari grasped Isobel's hands in hers. "I'm so pleased to make your acquaintance."

Charlie continued with a swat at Callum's chest. "And this oaf who so rudely awoke us is Callum MacDonell."

Callum greeted Isobel kindly then turned to Charlie. "Oaf, is it? Have a care. I ken things about you I might share if provoked." He glanced at Isobel, who smiled, but then turned to Charlie and lifted an eyebrow.

Only then did Charlie realize that his friends doubted his explanation and suspected there was something between Charlie and his travel companion. He would clear that up later.

They all sat down to share a breakfast of bannocks and ale, while Callum, Mari, and Bessie caught Charlie up on all of the changes that had taken place since he left. There were many. Babies had been born, people had died, couples had courted and married, and all the while, the land was worked, crops were grown, sheep were shorn, wool was spun, dyed, and woven, and folk gathered about the peat fires to sing and tell stories.

Life here was as he'd remembered it, simple and good. He leaned back in his chair and felt the deep content-ment of home mixed with grief over the loss of his mother.

As the morning sun traced a path through the window, Charlie learned that Callum's father, the laird of the castle, had died. Callum might have been laird, but he had given up his inheritance, and the arranged marriage that came with it, to be with his true love, Mari. Now his father was gone.

"Well, I'm sorry to hear it. He loved you. That much was clear."

"Aye. It was not always easy between us, but we grew close toward the end."

The thought settled for a moment as Charlie recalled Callum's difficult childhood as the illegitimate son of the laird. "So your cousin Ranald is laird now?"

"Aye." Callum looked pensive.

This did not escape Charlie's notice. Callum had made the decision for Mari and would never regret it. Even so, no one would blame him for wishing it had not been necessary.

Callum shook off his mood. "And Nellie. We miss her so dearly." He peered at Charlie. "I'm sorry you had to come home and find out this way."

Mari put a gentle hand on Charlie's shoulder. "We had no way to reach you. No one knew where you were— except that you were fighting in Europe somewhere."

"Aye, well, 'tis my own fault. I should have come home long ago."

Callum gripped Charlie's shoulder. "I'll take you to her grave later on."

"I've already been. I found it last night." Charlie's answer was so brusque that no one spoke for a moment.

Callum broke the silence. "Have you time to go fishing before you leave us again?"

Charlie's mood lifted. "Leave you again? I'll be gone for two days, perhaps three, and then I'll be back to stay. Until then, I'm sure that you'll manage without me."

"Oh, Charlie, we've missed you." Mari smiled with such warmth that Charlie could not help but be moved.

"I've missed you, too, Mari."

Callum cleared his throat. "Well, if you two dinnae stop missing each other, we'll have no time for manly pursuits. Bring Mistress Shaw to the house as soon as you're ready. She and Mari can get to know one another, while we find Alex and go to the loch."

"Duncan's still in Ireland, then?"

"Aye, he is."

"I suppose I was hoping..."

Callum shook his head slowly. "I'm afraid that he'll not be able to live in Scotland again."

Charlie returned Callum's knowing look. Their friend Duncan had encountered some trouble with a cruel British officer, and he'd fled with his bride, Jenny, to Ireland.

Callum's brow lifted. "He's done very well for himself there."

"Has he? Good for him."

"Aye, he's had a commission to privateer for some time and has amassed quite a fortune. He's talking of buying a second ship—solely for trade, so he says."

"So you've seen him?"

"Aye."

"And Jenny—is she happy?"

"Oh, aye, very happy."

Charlie found it too hard to speak. It was good to be home, and he felt it deeply.

While Isobel helped Bess and Mari with the dishes, Callum followed his friend's gaze to Isobel. Charlie did not take his eyes from her until she climbed the stairs out of view.

"She's a fine woman."

Charlie shrugged. "Fine enough, I suppose."

Callum's eyes danced.

The two men had been through too much for Charlie

to miss Callum's amusement. He pulled back his shoulders. "She's just lost her husband."

Callum was instantly somber, as well as intrigued.

Charlie explained what she'd been through then shook his head slowly. "'Twas only her spirit and an even greater measure of luck that saw her to the safety of a nearby cave. It was there that I met her."

Callum thought for a moment then lifted his eyes to Charlie's. "And what brought you to the cave?"

"Och, I was hiding."

Callum leveled a gaze. "Hiding from whom?"

Charlie looked a bit sheepish. "Well, at the inn where I stopped, there was a woman."

Callum lifted an eyebrow. "A woman?"

"And she had a husband."

Callum simply closed his eyes for a moment and shook his head.

Charlie held up a palm in defense. "It wasnae my idea. She followed me outside and, well, what was I to say?"

Callum looked at him frankly. "No?"

"No? Are ye daft, man? Had you seen her, you'd not have blamed me one bit."

"But her husband apparently did?"

Charlie sighed and looked upward. "Aye."

"Hence the chase?"

Charlie nodded helplessly. "And the cave where I met her."

"The woman?"

"No, Mistress Shaw."

Before Callum could probe further, the women returned, for which Charlie was grateful.

"So, Charlie, are you staying tonight?" Callum asked.

Charlie looked at Isobel before he answered, and she nodded. "Aye."

"Good," Callum said. "When we get back from fishing, we'll have a wee ceilidh. Bess, will you spread the word?"

Charlie opened his mouth to protest, but the others were already planning—except for Isobel. She met his eyes with a look that was knowing and kind, and it comforted him. The feeling was strange, and it forced the realization that no one had comforted him in a very long time. Until now, he had not thought he needed comfort. He now wondered how he had managed without it. Isobel looked away first, and the moment was gone. But it left an impression.

CHARLIE SAT by the cairn where his mother lay buried. It was the time in late evening when the summer sun was reluctant to set, and bits of clouds seemed to rise from the hills like plumes of smoke drifting by. Unshifting and solid, the hills had not changed. People had still lived and died in his absence, and the life he remembered was gone. Now he would look at the hills through memories that drifted by like the clouds, which he could neither reach nor hold onto. His brother had once played down in that loch, and his mother had often picked berries on the heath. Sometimes, his father would sit by the fire and tell old stories of life as it lived in his memories.

Charlie had no doubt in his mind that his mother's burial had been properly done and deeply felt by all who had known her. But everyone else had had several months to grieve and move on with their lives. For him, it had come as a blow worse than any that might strike him in battle, for this came in a time and a place that was supposed to be safe. It took him by surprise, leaving a deep and raw wound. He could barely keep it tamped down in the presence of others. But now on the hill by the kirk, alone except for the souls who rested there, he could grieve.

He inhaled the scent of the grass carried by the summer breeze. It smelled like home and the childhood days when he and his brother had run over these wild Highland hills without care. They had known these hills well and had loved them with hearts that were careless, not realizing how quickly such moments would pass. But the Highlands were constant and true to the people who lived there and tended the earth for a time.

Perhaps Hugh had been lucky, if only in one way. He had never come back to find everything had changed. As children, they'd fought their way over this land with swords fashioned from sticks they'd found on the ground. It seemed such a simple life now. Too young to know they would not be here for long, they had lived in a home filled with love. Clothed and fed, they did chores, got in trouble sometimes, learned their lessons, and grew to be men. There were no grand events in the life of a cotter, not when compared to the things he had seen as a mercenary soldier in Europe. No grand buildings like he'd seen in Paris stood here, nor were there statues as large as some buildings he'd seen. Here, wealth grew deep as the roots in the ground, and richness was found between families, friends, and the clan.

But his family was gone now, and he was alone. He

looked out and wondered why they'd been given such beauty to fill their senses and minds if it all ended in heartache. Perhaps beauty was their consolation. The heathery hills blurred before him, and he wept.

The sun had nearly set by the time Charlie stood, staring numbly. He sensed someone's presence, which was never a good thing to feel in a graveyard. He shivered. It was time to go home. He got up and turned. At the top of the hill stood a woman, whose clothing he knew in an instant. It was Isobel. Although too far for their gazes to meet, it was not too far to feel her concern. As he stood, she turned and walked back toward the croft.

Chapter 8

The Fall

Had they not been outside, the floor would have shaken beneath them from the force of the dancers. They moved in formation to the lively tune, played by a whistle, fiddle, harp, and bodhrán. But they danced beneath a bright moon. No star could hide on such a clear summer night. Charlie stood near the fire, whisky in hand, and stared at the flames.

Isobel thanked Alex's wife, Kenna, for sparing her husband for a dance. Charlie's friends had gone out of their way to make her feel welcome among them—much more so than Charlie had since they'd arrived. He was too lost in his grief. In truth, it surprised her to see that he had such deep friendships at home, for he'd made such a point these past years of wandering the world, unattached. But the affection they all shared was striking—as deep as a family's. He would need that now that his last family member was gone. He had taken the news with a stoic reserve, but he was not one to share painful emotions, at least not with her.

Isobel made her way to a comfortable spot where she could take in the music and watch the spirited people of Clan MacDonell. Before long, her eyes settled on Charlie, brooding into his whisky. She watched him with interest then had to remind herself that he was not hers to watch. As a woman in mourning, she should not have been dancing, either. Neither should she have been worried for Charlie. Whatever it was that was drawing her toward him was better left to someone else. He had friends and no shortage of bright-eyed women dancing about him—this evening, literally. But even as she admonished herself, she walked toward him.

"Charlie!" Bessie appeared and hooked her arm into Charlie's and tugged. "Come on! You've not danced once this evening."

Isobel managed to stop without attention from Charlie or Bessie, while Charlie replied in too quiet a voice to be heard. Bessie cajoled him until he gave in. Still holding his whisky, he looked about and caught Isobel's eye just as she was turning away. "Would you hold this for me?" he asked, with pleading eyes and a good measure of charm.

Feeling put upon, as though she existed to serve him, Isobel opened her mouth to protest. But the cup was in her hand, and the couple was off to dance before the right words came to mind.

"He's a good man—and good-looking, as nae doubt you've noticed."

Isobel turned to find Mari beside her. "Aye, he is." She hastened to add, "As are all of the MacDonell men." Her efforts to look nonchalant had failed miserably, as Mari's soft gaze made painfully clear.

"I've always thought of Charlie as a sort of fine wine who needed some aging before he'd be ready."

Isobel chuckled, but it was a half-hearted effort. "Ready for what?" She knew exactly what Mari had meant.

Mari's eyes sparkled as she smiled. "How can anyone help but adore him? He's like fresh air and sun, but there's more there than he'd want us to see. Charlie just needs some time."

Isobel nervously smoothed her fingers over the whisky cup she still held in her hand. "Aye, well, I'm sure he'll find the right woman."

Mari glanced at Isobel then watched Charlie dance with a soft smile on her face. "Bess isn't that woman."

Isobel turned with a startled expression, but Callum swooped in and swept Mari into his arms. "Will you dance with me, lass?"

Mari laughed and looked down at her very pregnant belly. "Callum, I cannae."

But he took her so tenderly into his arms and led her in a dance that was slower and dearer than any the others were dancing.

Isobel had once dreamed of a love like that. With a sigh, she turned to see Charlie dancing with Bess. She looked down at the whisky he'd left with her and shrugged. Tipping the cup, she emptied what was left in it and set the cup down on a rock that she passed as she walked to the outskirts of the crowd.

All she wanted was home, where she could grieve for a husband and the life she had barely known. And she could try to forget she had ever known Charlie—not that there was all that much to forget. She imagined that he'd kissed so many women in his life. The one they had shared was just one more kiss that meant nothing. Two lonely people had yearned to be close to whomever might make them feel human again. Touch could substitute quite well for caring. But when one person cared and the other did not, then it just made things worse. All she needed was to be home, where she could regain a proper perspective on things. At home, she would feel like herself once again. With that settled, Isobel exhaled the breath she'd been holding.

"Such a deep sigh, Mistress Shaw!" She flinched at the sound of Charlie's voice.

He laughed and put his strong hands on her shoulders. "'Tis only I. Have I frightened you, Isobel?"

"No, I just thought I was alone." She could not see his face in the moonlight, but that meant he could not see hers, either, for which she was grateful.

He said, "I'm sorry. I imagine it's not easy to be here amid so many strangers."

"No. That is, ordinarily no. But it's been rather difficult lately."

"Aye. I sometimes forget what you've been through—and that you're in mourning. And of course that means no dancing. But have I not seen you cheat once or twice this evening?"

"Aye."

He leaned close, and her heart quickened. "I'll not tell a soul."

Despite all of her efforts, she could not seem to get past Charlie's warmth toward her in moments like this. It was as though when they were alone, he was a different person—a person she had grown to feel at ease with whether they were talking or silent. This did not help her keep her feelings in check.

Charlie turned to her. "Would a wee dance, then, be such a terrible thing?"

"A dance?" All she could think of was how she would feel in his arms, and it terrified her. More and more, when she was with Charlie, good sense left her and feelings took over. And there went the ease she'd felt moments ago.

"Aye, a dance. You put your arms so, and I hold you just so, to keep you from falling when my clumsy feet get in the way." By the time he was finished, she was in his arms. The next moment, they were dancing in the shadows, where no one would see. If he got any closer, he would feel her heart pounding. Yet it was she who leaned closer to smell the scent she had grown so familiar with riding on horseback with him. Then there was the warm strength of his arms. She was lost. The dance ended, and Charlie released her. The night air felt cold. They were quiet together, and she was acutely aware of his presence. It was almost as if she could sense what he thought—or more dangerously, what he felt.

She was unable to take the charged silence any longer. "Your friends think very highly of you."

Charlie laughed. "I dinnae ken who you've been talking to, but you're clearly mistaken."

Isobel smiled. "'Tis not so much what they say as how they regard you. They care for you deeply."

He leaned closer, as though sharing a secret. "Aye, they're a fine lot. Dinnae tell them I said so. It'll go to their heads."

"I'll not mention a word." She looked down and

thought before looking back up at him. "Why did you stay away for so long?"

"Ah, well, I suppose you'd have wondered that sooner or later."

Isobel spoke softly. "Not until I got here and saw how everyone adores you."

He leaned back against a tree, looked up at the sky, and said nothing for a long while. When he finally spoke, his voice was quiet and low. "When my brother Hugh died, it was like I'd been stabbed with that knife, for the pain never left. I'd promised my ma that I'd look after him, and I failed."

"But how so if it wasn't your fault?" She started to put her hand on his shoulder but caught herself.

"Because he was my brother. And my mother—she'd never have said it—but she had to have wondered if I might have saved him."

"But Charlie—"

"I couldnae face the pain that I'd see in her eyes."

"You'd have been a comfort to her."

He shook his head. "Not I. I've never been good with such things."

"Such things?"

"Comfort... feelings..." With a shrug, he went on. "I'm a soldier. It's the one thing I was good at. I knew what was expected of me, and I did it. It was clear and predictable. And I belonged."

"But you've so many friends here." She smiled. "And the women adore you—all of them, so it seems." Her grin faded as she saw his eyebrows draw together.

He turned and looked soberly at her. "I've never misled anyone."

"I never said that you have." His concern made her feel awkward for having pointed it out. She'd meant it to lighten the mood, but it clearly had backfired.

"I'd never hurt anyone."

She peered into his eyes and assured him, "I know that, Charlie."

He went on as if compelled to convince her. "With women, I always made sure we both knew what it was— and what it wasn't."

"Have you never loved anyone?"

"Not in that way. I didnae want to."

Isobel understood. After her heart had been broken, she'd made sure it would never happen again. She had married without love to ensure herself a tranquil and orderly life. In time, there would have been children to love. Perhaps she and Charlie were not all that different.

"I suppose I've been running from my feelings for years," he said.

"'Tis easier sometimes."

He looked knowingly at her. "Aye, 'tis so." He hesitated, as though searching for just the right words. "But sometimes, I wanted to stop."

"But you didn't."

His mouth quirked at the corner. "No, I didn't."

Isobel peered curiously at him. "But you've come home. That means something."

"It means that I'm weary."

When she thought he wasn't looking, Isobel studied Charlie's face. Strong and kind, there was something about his demeanor that contradicted his words. "What is it you want?"

Charlie smiled wistfully toward the horizon. "The

same thing anyone wants: a home, friends around me, a place to belong."

Isobel tilted a quizzical face toward him. "Ah, but you've just told me you've been running from having to feel."

Charlie winced. "Aye."

Isobel leveled a skeptical look. "Do you know what I think? I think you weren't running at all. I think you were searching."

She could tell she'd struck a chord, but he did what he always did. He made light of it.

He reached out amiably and took hold of her hand. "If that's so, I've gone a long way to return home empty-handed."

Isobel looked down at his hand, which was not empty now.

Charlie looked down as well and was quiet for so long that Isobel thought she should leave. She must have moved, for as if sensing her thoughts, he tightened his hand about hers.

He stared at their two hands. "Perhaps I was searching." He released her and folded his arms while he peered into her eyes. "And what about you, Mistress Shaw? Have you been searching, too?"

She shook her head. "No." He'd come too close. She was not ready for him to see through her.

Something changed in that moment. Charlie took his time before speaking. "I wonder if sometimes the right things can happen at the wrong time."

Without warning, his words brought her emotions too close to the surface. She fought to ignore them with little success.

Charlie looked off in the distance. "When the right time comes, I will seize it, and I will be faithful and true."

She was struck by his unabashed passion. "I hope that you find what you want."

Charlie said nothing. The two stood side by side, watching the ceilidh. He reached over and touched Isobel's hand again then twined his fingers with hers.

The next moment, she slipped her hand from his and disappeared into the crowd.

CHARLIE WATCHED HER FLEE, and he knew he'd just done the same thing that had sent him similarly running so many times in the past. He'd opened his heart without thinking. He'd not planned it. He felt like a soldier left bleeding in battle, still breathing and believing there would be a tomorrow. But he did believe there would be a tomorrow, and he wanted Isobel in it. For he knew that tomorrow and all the days after, he would love her.

Charlie started to walk—where didn't matter. He needed to think. He'd become one of them—one of the men who'd fallen into the abyss, just like his friends before him. First it had happened to Callum, then Duncan, and apparently Alex, although that particular spectacle had happened while Charlie was away. Alex and wee Kenna? He still shook his head over that one. Every time he had watched a strong Highland soldier reduced to a helpless bundle of tender emotion, he'd smirked. Yet, if forced, he would have confessed to feeling a pinprick of wonder and hope. For whatever love was, it struck with a powerful force that sent otherwise sturdy men to their knees. Who was Charlie, therefore, to withstand it?

Chapter 9

The Shifting Wind

Isobel moved through the crowd that surrounded the dancers. Too flustered by Charlie's unexpected confession to see which direction she was going, she stopped to recall how to get back to the cottage. If she left now, she could return there before the others and escape to her box bed, shut the curtain, pull the covers over her head, and then... what? Sleep? That was unlikely. Think? Her head spun, but her heart felt much worse, which alarmed her. Charlie had captured her heart, much against her own will.

It wasn't fair. It wasn't fair at all. She had guarded her heart carefully for so many years, and along came this rake to destroy all her work. No matter. She would steel herself and regain her control. She would have tranquility and order. As long as she hid his effect upon her, she would go forward as planned, alone and in control. For no matter how it began, it could never end well.

Not long after their meeting, she'd formed a good sense of Charlie's manner with women. He was charming, and he was so well-practiced at it that it was effortless—

and perhaps, sometimes, unthinking. Because of that, he was different from the young man who had broken her heart. Such men appreciated their capacity to cause pain, but did so anyway out of selfish desire. Women who trusted that their hearts were true and their actions were noble soon learned that such men were neither true nor noble.

Charlie was different, for he would never deliberately hurt her. It would happen by chance, in a moment of trust and neglect, and a deep wound would follow. Oh, she knew Charlie's sort. They broke hearts. But this time, it would not be hers.

The wind shifted, sweeping a storm along with it. Isobel fought gusts of wind and swirling leaves as she made her way back through the rain to the cottage. She hated to make such an early departure. Charlie's friends had been so warm and welcoming to her. But the sooner the night ended, the sooner she would be on her way home. She fought to open the door, but the wind blew against it. She struggled, her hands on the iron handle, and then it flew open. She slipped inside as the wind pulled the door open until it struck the stone front of the croft. All of her thoughts were forgotten when she turned and reached out to close the door, only to find herself face-to-face with Charlie.

He turned and pulled the door shut, latched it, then spun around. "Are you all right?"

When she nodded, he took hold of her shoulders. "You're soaked through. You must get out of those wet clothes."

She looked skeptically at him. "Oh, aye, that's a brilliant idea!" She left him behind and made her way to the fire.

"Isobel." He caught up and reached for her, but she took a step back.

Her heart was not as resistant to him as she hoped she appeared. All she could think of was how she was a widow and nothing about this made sense. "I'm Mistress Shaw."

He did not take it as a reminder as much as an arrogant insult. "Very well, Mistress Shaw." He practically spat it out. "Stay as rain-soaked as you like. I'm to bed." He turned to walk toward his childhood bed from force of habit but pivoted back. "God's teeth, I sleep here on the floor."

"Charlie."

He leaned closer and glared. "Mr. MacDonell."

They stood eye-to-eye, at an impasse until Isobel sheepishly looked away first. "Look at us. I dinnae ken who looks more foolish."

He lifted a brow. "You do."

"Och!" She pushed him away with her palms, a reflexive move from a childhood spent with an older brother. He scarcely moved in response, making her feel all the more foolish for resorting to childish tactics. "I'm sorry." It wasn't easy to say, but she said it. She lifted her eyes to find his soft gaze squarely upon her, and it had a most unsettling effect.

"Mistress Shaw—"

"Oh, Charlie—I mean Mister—och, very well! You may call me Isobel. I only meant that I am still a widow." Her pounding heart threatened to ruin her newly poised facade. "What I mean is, I allowed myself to do things this evening that I shouldn't. I've no business dancing or—"

Or feeling what I feel. She hastened to change the subject. "Would you mind if I warmed myself first by the fire? My clothing is wet, and I'm cold."

As if he had awakened, Charlie finally spoke. "Aye, I'll go get some more peat." He paused at the door. "You really ought to get out of those wet clothes. I promise to wait outside until you let me in. Latch the door if you like." Without waiting for an answer, he left, and she did latch the door.

After hanging her airisaid and skirts on the backs of chairs near the fire, she donned a spare shift that Bess had loaned her to sleep in and wrapped a woolen blanket about her shoulders. Soon after, she went to the door to answer his knock.

"Come in, Charlie." She thought she detected a slight smile when she used his given name, or perhaps it was the fact that she was inviting him into his own home.

For a long while, they sat quietly by the fire.

Charlie stared at the flames. "Was that you earlier on the hill?"

"Aye. I was worried about you grieving alone."

"Thank you."

She lightened her tone. "Dinnae make too much of it. I also worry about stray dogs and wounded birds."

He smiled, but it quickly faded. "Seeing you there made me feel less alone." His mouth quirked at the corner. "We scoundrels have our moments."

She showed no hint of a smile. "Aye, you do. That's what makes you so dangerous." She stood, and Charlie followed suit. "Well, 'tis late."

But as she bade him good night and took a step past

him toward her bed, he grasped her hand. "I swear I'd not hurt you."

She looked into those piercing blue eyes. "Oh, Charlie. How could you not?"

The door flew open, bringing in a cool gust of night air and a very merry Bess. Their hands slid apart, and Isobel bade Bess a good night then escaped to her bed.

Chapter 10

The Toll

Charlie woke Isobel at dawn. They were soon on their way, riding through a thick blanket of mist that made their whole world soft and gray. Charlie was not one to talk a great deal in the mornings, even more so after the previous night.

Isobel was thankful for that, and for the feel of the cool Scots mist on her face, which somehow calmed her troubled heart. Now, only hours from her home, she and her heart would be safe by nightfall. Any sleep she'd had the night before had been fitful, plagued by thoughts of how she had come to this place in her life. Meeting Charlie had thrown her off balance until she no longer felt sure of her heart. But by the end of the day, she would be home, where she would put everything back in place. With that settled, her lack of sleep caught up with her, and she dozed on and off against Charlie's back.

Isobel was a loyal and trustworthy lass, or so her father had always said. Whether she had been that way from the start, she no longer recalled, but she grew up believing it until it became fact.

Marrying Gerard Shaw had been one of her finest moments of prudence. No one had forced her to do it. He had appeared one day, seeking her hand. With her parents now gone, it fell to her brother to offer his consent, which he did without hesitation. She'd resisted the notion at first, but Mr. Shaw had a fine home and a large tract of land, and he treated her well. There was no heart-pounding thrill in his presence, nor had she expected there to be one. He was solid and safe, which was all she had wanted. After an appropriate time, they would have children, whom she would love and raise as she had been raised. In the evenings, they would quietly sit by the fire.

It would have been a good life, but that life was gone. She had nothing left but her thoughts. At least those were still her own. But her thoughts were tormenting her now. She could feel Charlie's heartbeat as she lay against his back. She would miss his strong shoulders and the feeling of riding with him. She felt safe in a way she perhaps never had felt before. It was almost as if she belonged here with him. She knew better than that.

The breeze brushed his hair against her brow. It shone amber and gold in the sun, so different from her long, dark tresses. But his hair was nothing compared to his eyes that were as blue as a loch on a cloudless day. Forced to circle her arms about him while they rode, she had grown so used to touching him and breathing his scent that she feared she would miss it as if it were air that she needed to breathe.

THEY WERE RIDING through a thickly wooded part of the road when Charlie's back stiffened. He slid his sword from its scabbard and whispered, "Hold on." Isobel tightened her arms about his waist.

A sudden rustle of branches and twigs brought a trio of men from the foliage to block their path. The man in the center was imposing, with wild black hair. "You're on McLeod land now. There's a toll to pay here." He glanced at Isobel. "That surly wench will do."

Charlie reached protectively back to Isobel and gripped her knee for an instant—a move which did not escape the leader's notice. Charlie assessed his options, jaw clenched. He faced three sturdy warriors. Fighting them while keeping Isobel safe would be a challenge. He steeled himself to take on the first one who moved toward him.

"For pity's sake, John!" Isobel said. "Have you lot nothing better to do?"

The three men burst into peals of laughter.

Isobel's voice held no amusement at all. "Charlie, this is my brother John. And those two buffoons are his friends, Owen and Duff."

Charlie was not smiling, either. Had he had a pistol at the ready, he might have shot one of them before being informed of the joke. They might be sturdy fighters, but their judgment was poor. For Isobel's sake, Charlie forced a smile. "I'd best sheathe my sword, then."

"Or just hand it to me," she said dryly. "I've a mind to put it to use on my brother."

"Och, lassie, dinnae be cross. We were just having some fun."

"Mr. MacDonell has done a great kindness to me, so I'd suggest you treat him as the honored guest that he is."

"Sorry, Izzy," said John, sounding very well-practiced.

A slight grin teased the corner of Charlie's mouth upon hearing the nickname. He looked over his shoulder and whispered, "Izzy?"

This earned him a sharp glance from Isobel, who then returned her attention to John. "He rescued me and has brought me home safely. I owe him my life."

"Rescued you?"

Charlie turned to John. "I did nothing more than any man of honor would have done."

"But you did it, and for that, I am grateful," Isobel said.

John offered a proper nod to Charlie. "Well, then, I am in your debt for your service to my sister." He turned his attention to Isobel. "But what danger befell you that brings you home now?" With a glance in Charlie's direction, he added, "Without your husband."

On the ride to Dernebroch, Isobel told them of her misfortune and her husband's demise, which gave Charlie ample time to feel put in his place by her brother, who was well-attired and rode atop a fine horse.

In other circumstances, such a man as Isobel's brother would not have fazed Charlie, which begged the question, why now? There was no escaping the answer—because he cared about her, what she thought, and worse yet, how she felt about him. Her brother's opinion would be added to one side of the scale. Charlie suspected that he could not afford to lose John's good opinion, a suspicion which became clearer as Isobel paid Charlie no heed in the miles that followed.

Doubt overtook him until, by the time they arrived, he'd convinced himself that she had no feelings for him other than gratitude for the good deed he had done by bringing her home. Anything else that had passed between them could be dismissed as weak moments between two lonely people. As a newly widowed young woman, she had an excuse. As for Charlie? He shook his head. Pathetic. Yes, that summed it up nicely.

CHARLIE LAY on a comfortable bed in the room Isobel's servants had led him to after she'd gone off with her brother to talk in the solar. Tapestries were hung on three walls of the bedroom, giving the chamber a feeling of comfort and warmth, while the fourth wall had a window that looked out on the bailey. Forest-green bed curtains were tied at each post of the carved oak bed, and a small table by the window held a pitcher, a bowl, and a beeswax candle.

Charlie lay on the bed and stared up at the ceiling. How could he have been such a dullard? Since he'd met Isobel, he had taken the lead in all things on their journey. If his charm was his best quality, then strength and confidence came next. Sure that he understood women, he had patiently waited for her to give in to her feelings for him. He had made it abundantly clear how he felt about her. The only thing in their way now was time... or so he had thought.

But now she was home in her element, where she had her own strength and confidence—and no need for his charm. She had wealth and station, which he would never possess. It was therefore no wonder she had kept him at arm's length. What sort of future could she have with him? Why would she leave all of this for a croft?

He was weary, but he felt the impulse to ride home now, no matter whether his horse was up to the return trip on the same day or not. He could flee McLeod land then stop for the night. Surely, his horse could do that. A deep sigh escaped. Home would be nearer. But nearer still was Isobel Shaw, and for some reason, Charlie could not bring himself to leave her. Not yet.

A LOUD RAPPING disturbed Charlie's sleep. He sat up and called out a groggy, "Aye?"

A young woman's voice answered. "Sir, I've been sent to fetch you for supper."

"I'll be there shortly." He went to the basin, splashed water on his face, and combed his fingers through his thick, sandy hair. Minutes later, he stepped off the bottom step of a rather grand staircase and was led down a long, narrow hall to the great hall, which lived up to its name.

From across the room full of people, Isobel looked at him, and his breath stopped. She was lovely. Of course she'd always been lovely. But now she was clothed in a crimson silk damask gown that set off her dark hair, which was swept up simply, and loosely wrapped in a sheer gold silk scarf. He wanted to untie that scarf and let down her long hair to see it cascade over her gown, putting the silk cloth to shame. He imagined how smooth her hair would feel as it slid through his fingers.

Light from a nearby candle caught her eyes as she

smiled. The warmth of that smile was almost too much to take in. Had a servant not drawn his attention and escorted him to the empty chair beside hers on the dais, he might not have made his way there. As it was, he arrived heart pounding and breathless, barely able to manage a greeting.

She laughed, completely composed. "Well, good evening to you!"

Charlie offered a bow. "Forgive me. I see that I'm late."

"We've only begun. Please sit down." Her warm smile was intended to put him at ease, but it failed when he looked into her eyes.

He was accustomed to lovely women and had always been able to sense their attraction or, as sometimes happened, lack of it. Either way, he had always felt self-possessed in their presence. But now, it was as if Isobel's tranquility came at his expense, for he was irrefutably lost —so far astray from his world, yet not nearly within reach of hers. He could barely recognize the helpless lass he'd met under duress in a cave and dragged through the Highlands of Scotland. Then he inwardly groaned when he realized he'd brought the exquisite lady before him to his home to sleep in a peasant's box bed.

But she'd never complained.

He watched her converse with her brother beside her and speak with the servants. They seemed happy to see her. Why wouldn't they be? In their place, he would have been content just to bask in the warmth of her gentle smile. She suddenly turned to him. With one look, she undid every well-practiced conversational strategy he'd acquired in his travels across Scotland and Europe. Worse yet, not only was she in control of herself and of her surroundings—Charlie included—but he had the decided impression that she knew it.

"Mr. MacDonell?" He had taken a moment too long to respond, which only increased his awkwardness. He quickly pulled his gaze away and looked about the great hall, acutely aware that he had little business up here on the dais, except by her generous kindness... or pity. He'd been raised in a croft, and he knew his place well.

His friend Callum, the son of a laird, was out of the norm, for he'd bridged two worlds and eventually wound up in the finer. Once there, he'd welcomed his friends into his new society. They'd been through so much together that their bond transcended social station. War did that to men.

There was no such excuse for Isobel. She had done him an undeserved honor by seating him so, and she had to have known it. Her gracious ease told him so. It was offered, no doubt, in gratitude for his service to her. But it made his heart swell, when it had no business doing so.

Charlie MacDonell was in trouble—if trouble meant love. Hopeless, unattainable, irrefutably doomed love.

As the meal proceeded, Isobel cast polite looks and occasional words his way, but her brother kept her attention drawn elsewhere much of the time. He was clearly the younger, attending to her with respect and affection, which Charlie could not help but envy. He'd had a brother who had looked up to him. While Isobel's parents were no longer living, they had left a strong family behind them in this brother and sister. Seeing them together made him long for his family again. As that could not be, he still longed to be home, in the place of his memories. He did not belong here. He had finished his mission to bring Isobel home. When he looked past his own present discomfort, he could see her sense of peace. In this place, she could grieve for her loss and look forward to a new life alone, or with someone else.

In that moment, Charlie resolved to be well on his way before dawn the next morning. It was best for so many reasons, not the least of which was for Isobel. She had no need for Charlie. From moment to moment, he shifted from desperate desire to hopeless self-loathing. While in the latter state, he watched her talking to John and was struck with the realization that she was completely untroubled by Charlie. As much thought as he'd given to her, she offered him gracious kindness with such thoughtless ease that it made his heart ache. Aye, the sooner he was on his way home, the sooner he would feel like himself once again.

He looked away and focused his thoughts homeward.

"Charlie?"

Startled from his musings, he turned to find her soft brown eyes searching his. "Aye?"

"I'm sorry. I havenae seen John since the wedding. Please forgive me for neglecting you."

"Neglecting? Och! Not at all. I was... lost in thought."

"Serious thoughts, I can see."

"No." He offered a weak smile but added nothing. Before Isobel, he might have offered an engaging anecdote to amuse and deflect from his true feelings, but he could not seem to be false with this woman, and everything true in his mind would have been an overwhelming outpouring of needless emotion.

Her brother once more drew her attention. Charlie wasn't sure whether he wanted to pummel John or thank him. He chose the middle ground and did neither. But as the guests gradually drifted out of the great hall and the noise lessened, he began to catch bits of her conversation with John.

"It's too early for that," she said sharply.

Charlie was not proud of it, but he found himself leaning just a bit closer to listen. He could not hear John. The man needed to speak up.

Isobel gave her head a slight shake. "Love?"

The scorn with which she said it struck a blow to Charlie's heart.

She went on. "Why is it that you men can be logical and calculating in your marriage choices, yet you won't allow women the same?"

"Isobel," John said, cajoling. The word marriage was definitely spoken, along with some mention of clan Gordon. Piecing it together, Charlie didn't need a great mind to surmise that John was already planning Isobel's next marriage.

"Would you at least allow me a proper period of mourning?" she asked.

John scoffed. "How much can you grieve for someone you barely knew?"

"But that's not the point."

John laughed. "You're in love with him, aren't you?"

"John! Keep your voice down!" she whispered.

No, John, speak up.

Isobel barely turned toward Charlie, but that movement alone made his heart skip a beat, for it secured in his mind that he was now the subject of their discussion. He lowered his eyes to the slice of blackberry pie on his plate, which now drew his focus. He lifted his fork nonchalantly and took a few stabs at the crust.

"No, I don't love him, but that's not the point."

Charlie stopped, a fork full of pie at his mouth, and set it down as if in slow motion. In the throes of battle, he had experienced moments when time had slowed down until he could see an arrow or bullet come toward him. In the end, they had missed, or he'd moved just in time. But this time, the arrow struck and sank into his heart. The talk that had absorbed brother and sister had finished him off. *Good God, man, leave before you unman yourself.*

A clansman, who still bore the road dust from his journey, came into the great hall and strode up to the dais. Formal greetings completed, he made an announcement to his laird. "The castle and land are officially yours. You have won."

John slammed his fist on the table victoriously, but Isobel put a placating hand over his. "John, Murray MacQuarrie approaches."

"He can approach all he wishes, but he's on my land." His eyes lit as he turned and bowed his head. "Sir Murray. 'Tis good to see that you carry your defeat with such grace."

"My defeat?"

John made a meager attempt to suppress a smug smile. "Oh, aye. The Privy Council has ruled that Dernebroch Castle and the land it sits on are mine."

Taken by surprise at the news, and now visibly angered, Sir Murray MacQuarrie said nothing.

John's eyes danced as he folded his arms and leaned back in his chair. "Searching for the right words to congratulate me, are you?"

Not so amused as her brother, Isobel's eyes went from one to the other.

MacQuarrie's eyes were ablaze. "Oh, I have words for you, John, but I'll not say them in front of the lady."

"Now, Murray, dinnae fash. Come, have a drink." John waved for a servant to bring another cup and had a chair brought to the dais beside him. He waved his arm toward the chair for Sir Murray to join him.

To refuse would have been a flagrant insult, so Sir Murray sat down, as expected, and drank.

John eased up on his gloating. "'Twas a fair decision," he said softly. "Let's not let this cause ill will between our two clans."

Sir Murray let out a deep grunt, which John took as agreement, though Charlie doubted it was.

"What is it that brings you here, by the way?"

"Nothing now," said a tight-lipped Sir Murray.

"Och, well, 'tis good that you're here. We can put all this nonsense behind us. Stay the night and join us on our hunt tomorrow."

With an arched brow, Sir Murray took a moment to consider. "No, I'm afraid I must return home. Some matters await my attention."

"Another time, then." John smiled with ease as Sir Murray MacQuarrie finished his whisky in one gulp and excused himself to return to his home.

As a low hum of conversation resumed, Charlie stood. With a bow, he thanked his host for his hospitality then bade him good night. Leaving the hall, Charlie arrived at the foot of the steps that led up to his room. There, he paused. More than anything—except Isobel—he wanted some air, so he turned and went out to the darkened bailey. As he'd hoped, the fresh air cleared his head, if not his heart.

Chapter 11

For Duty

The summer's eve sky lit the way as Charlie walked to the shore and looked over the water to the Isle of Skye's Cuillin Mountains. Unexpected emotion seized him as he thought about the unending beauty of his homeland. He'd not realized how much he missed Scotland until he came home. As majestic as the Highlands were, it was more than their beauty that rooted him here. This was home, and no matter how far he went, he would always return. His soul was here, as were those who had come before and would come after. Such was the power of his homeland. Its mist-covered highlands and lochs, as well as its people, were home. It filled his heart to be back. Although the heathery braes and the deep, grassy glens took no notice, he was home, and that meant everything to him.

He sat down on one of the boulders that stippled the shore. The shoreline reached out to the sea, and the mountains beyond that stretched up to the endless expanse of the heavens. In the midst of it all, Charlie felt small and alone. His family was gone, and without them, his home was no longer the same. Although he was glad he'd come home to Scotland, a small part of him longed for the uncomplicated life of a soldier. He'd never needed to think beyond the next battle. He had been housed and fed. He'd had one job to do, and he'd done it quite well. Now he was faced with a life that needed to be put back together. He had friends, but they'd moved on to their own lives with families and left him behind.

"THERE YOU ARE!" Isobel sat cheerily down beside Charlie.

He turned only partway toward her and nodded. "Aye, so I am."

"You left so abruptly."

"I'm pleased to see you safe at home with your family, but 'tis been a long journey, and I'm a bit tired."

"Aye, well, sleep well tonight, for I thought we might go walking tomorrow. I'd like to show you my favorite places."

He lifted his chin and looked out toward the sea but did not meet her eyes. "I'm afraid I'm away for home in the morning."

"Oh." She had not meant to sound quite so disappointed, but it was too late to conceal it now. "Well then, perhaps before you go, we could—"

"I must leave very early." He practically barked out the words.

Her heart sank. "I see." There was no mistaking his meaning. He could not wait to be rid of this place or perhaps even her. She breathed in and assumed the pleas-ing, but formal, demeanor she reserved for her guests—which was all that he was, she reminded herself. "Of course you're eager to get home."

Charlie nodded and silently stared at the sea, while Isobel tried to think of what to say. Something was wrong, but she couldn't work out what it was. They'd barely spoken all evening. Every time she had tried to turn to talk with Charlie, John had interfered with a question or more conversation—if it could be called that. She'd begun to suspect he did so by design to distract her from Charlie. He was full of grand plans for her future, which was the last thing she wanted to talk about.

She might have handled the situation better if her life hadn't so suddenly spun out of control, but she was still reeling from that. And now John was talking of marrying her off to a Gordon. After all, they each had their duty. His was being a clan chief, while hers was to marry to strengthen alliances. It was all for the good of the clan. It was as it always had been. Why should she question it now?

Because something had changed, and that something was Charlie. Through him, she had caught a glimpse of a life that was more than just duty. He lived every moment with spirit and passion. He held nothing back. But if that were so, any feeling he held in his heart would have been expressed by now, which had not been the case.

Still, she wondered about things he had said. He had hinted at things, but her perception was shaded by feelings for him. She could no longer trust her own logic. And yet, there were times she did not mind her new loss of control. Her heart was alive with new feeling and purpose from having known him. Though she doubted he knew it, he had taught her to breathe in life—to fill her lungs with it as if it were air. Was that kind of life not for her, too? Could she not know happiness?

Her brother had seen the change in her, for he knew her too well. Before she had dared think it herself, John had voiced it. "You're in love with him, aren't you!" He'd accused her as if she had murdered someone. The next moment, he'd laughed and advised her to do what she wished with her cotter, but then to remember her duty. Oh yes, she would marry again, but it would not be for love. Desire and marriage were two different things.

"'Tis late." Charlie's words cut into her thoughts abruptly, startling her.

"Charlie—"

Before she could go on, he stood and offered his hand. "Forgive me. Of course I'll escort you safely inside."

She wanted to talk with him—to find something to say that would change things between them. He'd grown cold toward her since their arrival. She did not understand it, but truth did not need to be understood. Even now, when he'd taken her hand to help her up, she'd felt something between them. But along with it, she felt something that kept them apart. And that barrier kept her from sharing what troubled her now. So together, they walked through the cool night air, which was full of the unspoken words that would never be voiced.

They arrived at the foot of the stairs that led up to his room. Charlie lifted her hand and pressed his lips to it, then he lifted his eyes to meet hers. Her heart sank from the weight of unexpressed longing.

His eyes, soft and deep, searched hers. "Goodnight, Isobel." He then bowed and turned to go up the stairs.

Isobel turned away to escape, but he reached out and grasped her hand. She drew in a sharp breath as he pulled her against him and held her close enough that she could feel his heartbeat. Unable to help herself, Isobel looked up with unguarded emotion.

"Dear Isobel, dinnae marry for duty again," he said quietly.

It was as if she'd taken a blow to the heart, for his words assumed that she would, in fact, marry again. And they further implied that it would not be to him, and that was the part that took her breath. She could not let him see how he'd hurt her. "And why not marry for duty?"

"A loving marriage and family would fulfill you."

Bitterness started to burn through her eyes. "Would it? Then why aren't you married? From where I'm standing, your life looks as empty as mine."

Her triumph dissolved as she saw that she'd hurt him. With a raised brow, he nodded, acknowledging her point and its harshness. A truth flickered in his eyes but was gone just as quickly. "I only meant you deserve to be loved."

Her shock at his bluntness shielded the pain of its truth for a moment. "Some people aren't destined for love."

He regarded her as he might look at a stranger— almost from a distance. "Do you really believe that?"

Isobel fell back on words that she used to believe. "There are other things as important."

"Such as?"

She met his eyes plainly. "Doing one's duty, fighting

for what's right. Since you ask, what have you been doing these past several years?"

"'Tis a very good question, which I cannae answer. I could call it duty, but I would be lying. If it is duty, as I believe it is for some, when is it done?"

She opened her mouth but could not form an answer, so she shrugged. "Maybe sometimes, you just stop."

Charlie was silent and still.

Needing to fill the emptiness, Isobel went on. "You and I both have done our duties, and we've survived without love, have we not?"

The wistful look in his eyes brought her wounded heart back to life in a way that it shouldn't have.

With no warning, he gently took her face in his hands and planted a kiss on her forehead. "Aye, so we have."

Then he flashed the well-practiced smile that no doubt had charmed women all over Europe—and here. He bade her good-bye and bounded up the narrow spiral of stairs.

When he was gone from sight, she turned and leaned against the stone wall. "Dinnae marry for duty!" she whispered. Had he asked her, she would have thrown duty and her own good sense away and run off with him this very night.

But he had not asked.

She shut her eyes and sighed. Had she not sorted her thoughts and feelings out years ago? Although she had never understood why, she was the sort that men took from. Whether from her heart or her position in life, they took. But no man ever came to her wanting to give. Charlie had confused her, for he did give her something, which she would never forget. But he left her with heartache. It must have been some kind of sport, but the game had ended when he brought her home. Perhaps he was really no different from the others. It was she who had let down her guard. Although some had tried, no man had come close to reaching her heart until Charlie... because she had let him. And for that lapse in judgment, she'd earned what came next. *Good work, Isobel. You've just let that man break your heart. Weak moments have consequences, and now you'll live with yours.*

CHARLIE WAS WELL down the road before dawn. "You're off your head, gutless clod," he muttered as he rode away from Dernebroch. But he just couldn't face the final loss of his hope. Had it not been enough to look into her gentle brown eyes and see all that he longed for? His love shone back at him from her eyes. And that was what hurt him the most, for he'd seen a glimpse of her heart, and that fleeting glimpse had made him feel whole.

In an instant, he knew what made men give over their hearts and their lives to the women they loved. Until he'd met her, he believed he was not meant for love since he'd never known it. He'd even become quite content with his lot. He'd accepted as fact that he loved women too much to settle on one. But then he met that one. Here was a woman who deserved to be loved. And he wanted that love to be his.

Wanting was not always having. Apparently, Isobel knew that better than he. A woman of Isobel's station could not live the life Charlie offered. Had he not caught snippets of things her brother had said, no doubt intending to be overheard? With her husband only just buried, her brother was already working to secure the next one, and he was not about to let Charlie ruin his plans. Isobel's future was set. It did not include Charlie.

Why had no one ever told him that love was like being struck down in battle, except your senseless body kept walking about?

CHARLIE ARRIVED home to find Bess had moved out and returned to her childhood home with her brother and his wife. Well, that was one problem solved. She could not have remained without causing a scandal. Had she not gone, he would have had to seek refuge with Callum until they could have sorted matters out. Bess had kindly moved out, so now Charlie was home.

Weeks passed, and Charlie busied himself putting his home back in order. Repairs had gone undone for the years he'd been gone, so there was no shortage of work. Days blended from one to the next, but his heart did not change. He had hoped his feelings for Isobel would have faded, but his torment only grew stronger. As on so many days, he was cursing his fate as he mucked out the stables.

"I've brought you a mutton pie." Bess stood in the doorway, pie in hand, smiling.

Charlie grinned. "You're too kind, lass."

Bess searched his eyes. "I thought we might share this. Or have you eaten already?"

He leaned on his pitchfork and smiled, but his usual charm was tinged with regret. "I'm afraid I've a few things to finish." When she made no move to leave, he added, "You'd best not wait, as I may be a while."

She did not hide her disappointment well. "Another time, then. I'll just put this inside on the table."

"Bess! Thank you. 'Twas a kind thing to do."

She lingered for a moment, then gave a nod and headed for the house.

Charlie watched her then shook his head as he turned and scooped up more hay with the pitchfork. Her cooking was fine, but it came with a price—and that price was her heart, which he could not accept. Of all the women he'd known, there was one sort he avoided. They had a look that could not be mistaken, and Bess had that look of a woman in love.

Perhaps it was time he paid Callum a visit. He could make himself scarce for a few days or so—long enough for Bess to find some other place for her heart to bide. And what better time was there than now?

Chapter 12

The Long Night

A young housemaid opened Callum's front door. "Oh, Charlie, it's you. 'Tis the mistress. The bairn's coming early."

Charlie strode past her to the study, where Callum and Alex were devoting themselves to a decanter of whisky. Alex poured Charlie a glass then refocused his attention on Callum. They'd known Callum all of their lives. They'd been through battles and brawls together. It was Callum who had always been in control. Nothing ever fazed him—until now.

Callum swallowed what, judging from his distracted appearance, could not have been his first drink. "Alex, would you go check on her?"

"Aye." He gave Charlie a knowing glance and left.

Callum looked up at Charlie with so forlorn an expression that Charlie wanted to laugh. "They've sent me away. I'm forbidden upstairs. I'd take on anything— anyone—without fear. Except this. Now I'm to sit here with nothing to do while she suffers up there."

Charlie had watched Callum fall in love, and he knew that Mari was his life. But women had babies, and a man had to get through it like other men had done for generations before him. So Charlie smiled and refilled Callum's glass. "She's not the first woman to give birth."

"No, but this isnae her first," Callum explained. "She's lost two, and I'll not watch her heart break again."

Charlie knew better than to offer false hope to Callum. The best thing he could do was be there beside him, no matter what happened.

Alex walked in. "She's a braw one—Kenna's words, not mine." He offered an encouraging smile. "She's doing well."

A round-faced young servant appeared in the doorway, holding a very tired young girl with wild, fire-red hair by the hand. "She's ready for a nap but wanted a hug from her da."

The child shot an inquisitive look at Charlie then settled her gaze upon Alex.

"Come here, little lassie." Alex scooped the girl into his arms and planted a kiss on her cheek. "Would you like to meet Charlie?"

"No," she said with a child's honesty.

Charlie gave her a crooked grin. "I have that effect upon women."

Alex hugged her once more. "Sweet dreams, my wee one," he said before sending her back to the housemaid with a pat.

"Does she have a name?" Charlie asked, still not used to the fact that Alex was a father.

"Gillian." He turned to Callum. "I cannae believe it's

been three years since I sat outside my cottage and waited as you're waiting now."

Callum combed his fingers through his hair. "'Tis been three hours."

Alex's mouth twitched at the corner. "We might have a long night ahead. Shall I find us some food? Everyone seems to be upstairs, but I'm sure I could find something to stave off the hunger."

Callum shook his head absently and leaned back in his chair, while Charlie's eyes brightened.

As Alex left the room, Callum exhaled and looked at Charlie. "Tell me something to distract me."

"I've not much to tell. I'm glad to be home, but in truth, the croft feels empty."

Callum smiled. "Well, if you hadnae sent poor Bessie away..."

"I did no such thing. But I would have if she hadnae gone on her own." Charlie paced about, trying to walk off his frustration.

For the first time today, Callum smiled. "You're the one who's lonely."

"I never said lonely. I said empty—the croft feels empty." Charlie sank into a chair.

"I hear Bess has her eyes on you."

Charlie looked up at Callum, unamused. "Well, her eyes can look elsewhere. God's teeth, Callum, if you knew me at all—"

Callum grinned and protested. "I'm merely pointing out what you're too blind to see."

Charlie set down his whisky. "Which is what?"

"That she fancies you."

"Do you ken who you're talking to, Callum?" He realized Callum was baiting him, but he could not help being annoyed.

Callum chuckled. "Then you've not lost your senses completely."

"My senses are fine. I'm just not keen on Bess."

Callum shook his head. "She's a fine lass."

"For someone—not I."

"In all seriousness, Charlie, surely by now, you must have some idea of the sort of lass who would be for you."

"I do."

"Good! Now we're making progress."

"I've met her."

Callum leaned forward and slammed his palms on the desk. "'Tis a miracle." The more Charlie glared, the more Callum laughed. "So... who is she?"

Charlie, by now, had lost patience. "Well, who do you think?"

Callum grew suddenly serious. "I think... that you could not mean—"

Charlie nodded. "Isobel Shaw. Aye." He held up his hand. "Dinnae say it. I know. She's a fine lady, who lives in a castle, and I'm a crofter. And that is the end of the story."

"Except that you love her."

Unable to bear the pitying look Callum gave him, Charlie leaned forward and stared at his hands. "I didnae choose to love her."

Callum's eyes shone. "Do we ever choose love?"

"No." Charlie shook his head dismally. "Love's more like a flood. Try though we might to deny it, it rises and washes our good sense away just before its overpowering current carries us off to our fated demise."

A crooked smile formed on Callum's face. "I suppose that's one way to look at it."

"Aye." Charlie could not have been more forlorn. "But I love her."

From the main entryway rose a commotion, prompting an already edgy Callum to bolt to his feet. He was halfway to the door when a tall, travel-worn man walked in. "God's teeth! Duncan?"

Charlie sprang up. "And Jenny! But who's this?" Charlie bent down and lifted a boy who could not have been much more than two. With his black hair and eyes nearly as dark, there was no mistaking he was Duncan's.

The boy gave Charlie a guileless look. "Hughie."

Charlie's expression went blank as he swallowed back the emotions that rose with no warning. While he was away, he'd heard Duncan and Jenny had had a son, but no one had mentioned the name. Years had passed, but thoughts of his own brother, Hugh, were never too far away.

Jenny put a gentle hand on Charlie's shoulder. "Do you mind?" she tenderly asked him.

In the meantime, Callum and Alex had stopped and watched Charlie intently.

"Mind? No!" He recovered his usual cheer and tousled the boy's dark hair as he looked at him and smiled. "'Tis a fine name for a fine lad." He glanced at Duncan and gave him an affirmative look that spoke the words he could not presently voice.

Collective relief seemed to settle over the room as they settled into chairs and warm conversation.

JENNY HAD GONE UPSTAIRS to help Mari by the time the candlelight flickered on the four dozing men in the study. A faint cry came from above. Callum bolted upright. "Did you hear that?"

Charlie stirred and began to awaken.

Without waiting for an answer, Callum rushed out of the study and took the stairs two at a time. The midwife met him outside the door with a chastising, "Shh."

Like an errant boy, Callum calmed himself down and stepped quietly into the bedroom. His eyes softened as he took in the sight. Mari lay sleeping with their newborn in her arms. He paused to swallow back his emotions. Before him lay all that mattered in the world, and his heart filled so much that he thought it might break. A fleeting moment brought Charlie's description of love to his mind, and he smiled. Love had, indeed, swept him away with its power.

He sat down on the edge of the bed and leaned down to touch his lips to Mari's forehead, while the baby's tiny hands flexed in surprise. Mari opened her eyes and smiled wanly. "Callum, look. Is she nae bonnie?"

"Aye, lass, like her mother."

Chapter 13

The Fortress

"Look at you. A fortnight has passed, and you pine for him still," Isobel said to herself as she leaned her elbows on the stone windowsill and watched the brooding gray clouds tumble over the hills.

Somewhere out there was Charlie, content in his home. All his friends were nearby, including that Bess. Surely upon his return, he would not bide with her in that croft all alone—not that Bess would object. She had made little effort to hide her feelings for Charlie. A wave of jealousy rose up to torment Isobel, but she tamped it back down. It was not like her to give in to emotions like that. She had no hold on him. He owed her nothing.

In truth, he'd done more for her than many men would have. With unerring kindness, he had escorted her safely to her home, and with that done, they'd parted. Any feelings that might have passed between them were never meant to be, let alone continue. Life was full of fleeting glimpses of what might have been—moments nearly within grasp, and then gone—leaving only a heart that was helplessly pounding until it slowed to an ache. She thought perhaps he'd felt something for her as well. But what did it matter when the moment was gone? That was why she had worked all these years to keep romantic feelings in check. She had erected such a fine fortress around her heart, only to have all her work toppled by a man in mere days, and with what looked like no effort. Foolish heart. Would it never grow wise?

A lone rider came into view. For one breathless moment, she hoped it was Charlie. But as the man drew nearer, she recognized Roddy, one of the lads who fostered with her brother. They'd all gone off hunting early this morning. The fact that he rode back alone was enough cause for concern, but even more so as he rode with such haste and cried out to the sentries to raise the portcullis.

Alarmed, Isobel rushed downstairs and made her way out to the bailey. "Roddy, what is it?"

He struggled to catch his breath. "We were hunting."

"Aye, Roddy, I ken you were hunting. What happened?"

"A large party of MacQuarries came out of the trees and ambushed us. I'd gone off to the shrubs to, well, you ken, so I was able to get on my horse and ride off. They tried to shoot me, but I got away."

Isobel gripped his shoulders and peered into his eyes. "And the others?"

"I didnae linger to see. I'm sorry, but there were too many. I couldnae fight them myself."

"Of course not. But tell me what happened next."

He stared at her in helpless silence and shook his head.

Isobel could barely quell her frustration. "Any more

shots?" She gripped his shoulders and shook him. "Did you hear any more shots?"

"No." He squinted, recalling. "No more shots were fired."

"Then they must have been captured."

"Aye, I suppose so. Elsewise, they'd be on their way home close behind me."

Thoughts raced through Isobel's mind. "If they've been captured, they've been taken to Castle MacQuarrie to be held in their dungeon."

Roddy nodded. "Aye, I suppose."

Isobel glanced about at the few men left guarding the castle. "Then there'll be a ransom demand—or worse. We'd best brace ourselves." As concerned as she was for her brother, anger mounted within her. He'd taken so many men with him that he'd left the castle vulnerable to attack.

Since their father had died, there had been a brief period of unrest when neighboring clans had sought to usurp John as chief. The attempts had been promptly put down by the strong clan loyalty their father had established over the years, and by John's unyielding might. But in the past few years, men had gone off to fight Covenanters or to seek far-off battles as mercenary soldiers in Europe. Peaceful years had followed, and John grew complacent. Now his greatest challenge was to outdrink his friends as they worked their way through the barrels of whisky in the cellar. Since young Roddy had arrived, he'd learned more about carousing than handling a sword.

At this point, there was naught to be done about that. Isobel made a quick mental count of the men. No more than a dozen—a few trained to fight, who were well past their prime, a blacksmith and a few other tradesmen, a handful of servants, some farmers, and their women and children. Her eyes darted about as quickly as her thoughts. There was no time to waste. The MacQuarries were coming, and they had to be ready. This odd assortment of guards, tradesmen, women, and children would have to prepare. But who would lead them?

No sooner had the thought formed in her mind than she set about giving orders. "Start some fires. Fill all the buckets with water and bring them to the bailey. Fill every cauldron and cooking pot so they're ready to boil." She assigned men and women to oversee this task, then she moved on to some others, commanding them to gather arms and ammunition. The young and able-bodied women were instructed to find men's clothing to wear. "We may not have many men, but at least we can look like we do." Those unable to fight set about with the younger children, making straw men to place about the towers and ramparts.

By the time a messenger arrived, they were ready.

"Clan MacQuarrie has taken your laird and six men prisoner, to be held until you relinquish your claim on this castle."

Isobel called out from the tower. "You're on McLeod land, as it always will be! The Privy Council has declared it, and you'll never have it."

Young and brash, the messenger laughed. "You're a braw lass, to be sure, but you seem to forget that we've got your men."

"You can have them! But if one man is harmed, I'll come after yours, one by one, starting with your chief."

The messenger chuckled. "Now, lassie, your men are

all right—for now. But you'd best think what you're doing before you leave us with no choice."

The messenger's cocky grin faded to a scowl.

Isobel narrowed her eyes and lifted her pistol. She looked down the barrel. "Now I suggest you get off McLeod land before *you* leave *me* with no choice."

Off he rode, and Isobel watched, looking strong and unyielding. She only hoped no one saw how she trembled.

WHILE THE MEN and women boiled water and gathered their arms, Isobel set the children to work, gathering rocks and peat for the fires. They had ammunition and arms, but not everyone knew how to fire them.

One of the crofters' wives shook her head. "'Tis not right for the children to be put to work so. They ought to be safely hidden until this is over."

Isobel leveled a look at the crofter's wife. "If we do, they willnae be safe, even after it's over. We need every person. Do you not understand?"

"But they're children!"

"And children need families and homes." Isobel took a deep, calming breath. "You may take charge of the children. Take the wee ones down to the cellars and hide them there. I'll send the others down when they've finished their work here."

Still not entirely pleased, the crofter's wife turned and did as she was told. A man grumbled about taking orders from a woman, but Isobel put an end to such talk. "You're on McLeod land, and I'm in charge. You may stay or go as you wish, but the source of the orders won't change."

A few sideways glances were shared, but the people got on with their work.

A DAY PASSED as the clan readied themselves for the impending attack. When night came, Isobel gave in to advice to get sleep, for she would need it on the morrow. Closing the door to her chamber, she went to the window and flung it open to feel the cool air brush her face. "Oh, Charlie, where are you? You would know what to do, for such matters are easy for you. But for me, they are not. I will do what I think must be done, but will it be the right thing to do? People think that I'm strong, but I'm not. I have fooled them, but tomorrow, the truth will be shown. If I'm wrong, I'll accept my own fate, but I fear for my people and whether my choices will be their undoing. Perhaps that is the fate of all leaders to survive—or perish —knowing your error in judgment caused grievous misfortune to people you love. Always, I've sought what is best for our people, and I believe that is what I do now. I pray God it is enough."

HOURS LATER, Isobel awoke to a soft thud on the window glazing. She shot up in her bed and rushed to the window to look down below. A bird lay on the ground, dead or dying. She gasped. It was a bad omen. She stared into the sky, whose predawn light had not yet reached the ground. Darkness still clung to the earth like a shroud.

"It will happen today."

By MIDDAY, they had gathered every man, woman, and weapon they could. Then they waited. The air crackled with a mixture of expectation, aggression, and a fear that no one dared admit.

In the distance, three dozen MacQuarries approached, carrying swords and firearms, and hauling a battering ram, carts full of rocks, and a small trebuchet. They stopped a short distance away, and Sir Murray approached. "Mistress Shaw, have you considered our offer?"

Isobel stood tall and looked down from the ramparts. "Your offer to surrender our home and our land? Aye, I have, and the answer is no!"

He shook his head. "Bonnie lass, how it would grieve me to see that face harmed."

Her lips spread to a warm smile. "Would it really? I have no such fear for your face." Laughter erupted from the McLeod side of the castle.

"And what of your brother? Is this what he would want?"

A broad smile bloomed on her face. "I've not asked him. He's not home at the moment."

"He'd not wish to see his castle destroyed."

Isobel casually leaned on the stone wall and looked down at Sir Murray. "Well, then, he's in luck, for he'll not see what happens, will he?"

"My lady, may we speak?"

"I believe that is what we are doing, Sir Murray," she said, still smiling.

His eyes narrowed, but his voice remained smooth and pleasant. "In private?"

She considered his request for a moment, then turned and went down from the tower. She asked one of the few trained guards she had to stand by the gate at the ready. The portcullis opened, and out she went.

Sir Murray greeted her warmly, which under the circumstances did not sit well with Isobel.

"Sir Murray," she curtly replied.

He took his time, much to Isobel's annoyance.

"My lady, I was saddened to hear of your late husband's passing. I ken that it's soon, but I propose a solution to both of our problems."

"Our problems?"

"I am in want of a parcel of McLeod land, and you are in want of a husband."

"Sir Murray, I cannae imagine what gave you that impression. I am not—"

He interrupted. "I have made a good fortune in cattle and other ventures. I offer you marriage—you would want for nothing—in exchange for a wee tract of land—not the whole of it, but a parcel big enough to use when I bring cattle to market from Skye."

Isobel studied Sir Murray with interest. "Do I understand you correctly? Are you offering to marry me for the sake of your cows?"

He cleared his throat and stammered for the right words. "Well, I wouldnae put it that way. I need a place to corral them."

"And in exchange, you'd corral me?"

"Madam, you misunderstand."

"No, I believe I understand fully."

"Lady Isobel—"

"Sir Murray. As flattered as any woman would be to

enter into a negotiation on equal footing with a cow, I'm afraid I must decline."

"No, that's not—"

"Good day, Sir Murray." She turned and started for the castle, but Sir Murray called to her. With what little patience she had left, she turned back to face him.

"I beg you to reconsider, or you'll leave me no choice but to proceed."

She lifted her chin. "I will not. This is our land and our home. The Privy Council has declared it. Attack, and you'll not only answer to us, but you'll answer to them." Eyes blazing, she turned and walked through the gate.

"You'll regret your decision this day," Sir Murray called out.

"I will never regret it!" she yelled back as the portcullis lowered. She quietly added, "God help me if that isn't true."

THE MACQUARRIE ATTACKERS positioned themselves within range and, shielding themselves behind carts and armaments, began with a volley of arrows. Isobel crouched down behind the rampart wall with her archers —two boys, who were fostering there.

"My lady, there must be two dozen archers."

"Courage, lads. They can only fire one at a time, as can you. Aim and fire. All you need to do is hit one at a time." She looked him in the eye and gave a bolstering nod.

The boy grinned and turned to fire again.

Using a volley of arrows for cover, the MacQuarries

advanced their battering ram. Seeing this, Isobel ordered her men and women to cease firing. Met with questioning looks, she said, "Ready the cauldrons and let them draw close. We're no match for their arrows, but we can stop what can best breach the castle." Under her breath, she said, "And we've but a week's ammunition. We must make it last."

Isobel made her way to one of the towers that rose up beside the castle gate. When she saw that the battering ram was in place, she made eye contact with two women who manned a cauldron of boiling water. As the men neared the gates with the battering ram, Isobel gave a nod, and the women poured boiling water down the murder hole until their attackers cried out. Isobel turned and pressed her back to the wall to avoid the sight of the scalded men.

A crofter's wife approached Isobel. "'Tis the only way. We must fight for our homes."

Isobel looked at the woman she'd known since childhood.

With a straightforward look, the crofter's wife gave Isobel's shoulders a squeeze and went to retrieve a cooking pot that was boiling.

The MacQuarries retreated to a safe distance and regrouped. Before long, the trebuchet was in place and ready to fire.

"Find a safe place for cover until they draw closer," Isobel called out. Then she quietly added, "For I know nothing else we can do."

So they cowered as boulders flew over the wall, and some into it, leaving chips and dents in the wall, but no stones were dislodged yet. The barrage continued for over an hour, one strike after the other. How long could they withstand such assaults? Hours? A few days, perhaps? But what then?

Isobel and a half dozen villagers sat in the tower and waited. It had been quiet for some time, so she started to rise to steal a look down below. But something else drew her attention. "Do you smell smoke?"

At the same moment, the others noticed it, too. It came from the other side of the tower. The blacksmith looked out the window. "My lady, they've dug under the wall and have lit a fire. I'll get water."

Isobel turned to the others. "Gather all you can to bring water."

The cold water was poured on the inside, while three pots of boiled water were thrown on the outside, just missing a miner as he scurried back to the MacQuarries.

With the fire out, Isobel found the village stonemason. "What now?"

"They've weakened the wall. I cannae say by how much."

Isobel nodded and looked about as she thought. "If they can bring down the castle so easily, we might as well just open the gates and invite them inside."

The stonemason shook his head. "We can bolster the wall where they've weakened it."

"But how?"

"We usually gather the rocks from a quarry."

Isobel looked away. "We dinnae have a rock quarry inside the castle walls." Then she smiled. "But we do have some rocks."

He looked at the boulders that the MacQuarries' trebuchet had launched at them. He nodded and grinned.

"Tell everyone to gather the rocks and boulders and bring them to you," Isobel said. "How long do you think it will take?"

"Well, to do it right—days."

"And how long to do it well enough for now?"

"A few hours. We could fill in what they've mined well enough to hold for a while."

Isobel imagined the castle wall collapsing in a great cloud of dust. "How long is a while?"

"Perhaps a few weeks. We've enough here to hold up the wall until then, when we can make proper repairs."

"Good." She smiled and sent him on his way, but she wondered how long they would be able to defend against more undermining. "Best not think of that," she said with a sigh before heading back up to the tower.

As she mounted the steps to the tower, a loud boom resonated throughout the stairwell. Even before she could look out to see, she knew the MacQuarries were ramming the gates once again. But as she stepped into the tower, the women were pouring cooking pots of hot water on the men down below. The men cried out and retreated.

A woman returned from the window, empty pot in hand. "My lady, what will we do if we run out of water?"

Isobel's first instinct was to tell her to simply draw more from the well. Then her heart sank as she recalled that the well sometimes went dry in the summer. When it did, they'd always been able to gather the water they needed from the stream near the castle. But that stream was cut off to them now. If they withstood being rammed, mined, burned out, and shot at, they would be cut off until they starved to death or surrendered.

Chapter 14

The Drummer

After a week of gray days and drizzle, the clouds gave way to blue sky, drawing everyone out. Duncan swung Hugh up onto his shoulders as he, Callum, his family, and guests strolled along the path to the water. Spreading out blankets and setting down baskets of food, they sat down to enjoy the sun's warmth while they ate their midday meal. Mari rested her head on Callum's lap while Duncan taught Hughie and Gillian to fish. Seeing Gillian well-settled with Duncan, Alex leaned over and whispered something in Kenna's ear that drew a sly smile, and the two wandered off arm in arm.

Charlie leaned back on his elbows and smiled. His friends were all settled and happy—with children, no less. There was something stable and comforting here that he'd missed all the years he'd been gone.

Gray clouds drifted in, putting an end to their warm afternoon. They packed up and headed back to the house, while they argued about who would beat whom at chess.

Crossing the road, they came across a drummer with a cart of goods he was selling. He was a talkative man—perhaps that came with his trade—which afforded him much time alone. He was eager to chat and share the latest news while they all looked at his inventory. Mari examined some cloth for a quilt to warm the baby in winter.

Charlie glanced through the cart's contents but found nothing he needed. While he waited, he talked with the drummer. "Where have you come from?"

"The coast. It appears that I've brought the clouds with me." He chuckled a little too long, as soon became clear was his habit.

"The coast, you say?" Charlie hesitated to ask more, for he knew it would bring on some teasing from his friends, but he could not help himself. "Have you been near Dernebroch?"

"Oh, aye. But I couldnae stop—not with the castle under siege like it is."

"Dernebroch Castle is under siege?"

The alarm in Charlie's voice brought all other speech to a halt. His friends all looked on, concerned.

"Oh, have you not heard?" The drummer proceeded to recount all he knew, and a little bit more, of the siege of Dernebroch.

"You were there?" Charlie stepped so close, the old man straightened up in defense.

The drummer was a man who enjoyed telling stories in his own way and in his own time. "I was in the next village, and sales were good. 'Tis a nice place with good folk. Well, we were havin' a blether—"

"Aye, get on with it. What happened at Dernebroch?" asked Charlie, barely containing his frustration.

"Oh, aye. Well, I mentioned I was on my way to Dernebroch, when one of them warned me to stay away. They said the MacQuarries had had their eye on that land for some time." He looked at Charlie as though he were sharing a secret. "'Tis a very strategic location."

Charlie nodded quickly. "And the castle—its people— how did they fare?"

The drummer's brow furrowed. "Oh, aye. Well, I took their advice and didnae go there, so I dinnae ken how they are now."

While Callum thanked the old man and paid for the material and sundries that Mari had bought, Charlie left for the house.

Callum caught up with him in the stables. "Take a moment to think what you're doing." He put a hand on Charlie's shoulder, but Charlie shook it off and faced him, eyes burning.

"She's been under siege on her own for a fortnight. How can I tarry when she needs me?"

"Do you think you can fight off a whole clan single-handed?"

Charlie tightened the cinch on the saddle. "Do you think Isobel can?"

"Charlie—"

"Save your breath. I ken what you're thinking."

"I dinnae think that you do."

"You're thinking the same thing I'd think if I were standing there."

Callum leaned on the stall with a wistful smile. "I was once in your place—or have you forgotten?"

"Aye, I do seem to recall a lovesick fool storming into an illegal kirk meeting to steal a bonnie young woman away." In silence, each man was lost for a moment, recalling the things they'd been through together.

"Do you love her?" Callum asked simply.

There was no point in evading the question. "I do."

"Then you must go to her."

Callum turned, but Charlie put a hand on his arm to stop him. "It's not the same as it was with you and Mari. We'll not marry. She could never marry a crofter."

Callum did not argue the point, nor would anyone else have. Their difference in classes was too wide. Instead, he asked, "Does she love you?"

Charlie shook his head. "There are times when I think that she might. Sometimes I feel something between us. Och, but she's too strong to let herself love the wrong man. And I am that man."

"But you'll go to her now."

"Aye, I will," Charlie answered without hesitation.

Callum shrugged. "Then I'll go get the others."

CHARLIE WAS ON HIS HORSE, ready to go, as the men bade their wives good-bye. The women held their men in their arms as though it might be the last time they would feel their husbands' strong embraces. Then they stoically watched their men leave, while the children smiled and waved, unaware of the danger their men rode into.

The distant peaks ahead were nearly lost to a hazy sky that promised rain. Already, the dampness was settling in as the clouds drifted closer. The mist brought out the rich greens of the grasses and rough patches of foliage in the glen below, while a falcon dove swiftly and struck a duck, driving it to the ground with its merciless talons. It served as a reminder that raw beauty came at a price. Anyone who lived here did not forget that the Highlands were as harsh and unforgiving as they were stunning and grand.

With their home and their families well out of sight, Callum was the first to speak. "So, Charlie, what is your plan?"

Charlie offered a most sensible look. "Well, for starters, to form one." His mouth turned up at the corner. Alex and Duncan exchanged amused looks.

"Well, then, you're further along than I thought you might be," Callum said.

Charlie reached over to swat him, while everyone had a good laugh. Then they set about forming a plan.

"The MacQuarries are our allies, though tenuous ones," Callum said. "If we storm in to rescue your fair maiden, they might take it the wrong way."

"Oh, I think they'll take it precisely the right way." Charlie's frown soon followed. "But I dinnae want to put you in an awkward position."

Callum threw back his head. "Murray MacQuarrie's an arse. Someone needed to put him in his place. I wasn't planning on it being me, but since the occasion's arisen, carpe diem." He gave a reassuring look to Charlie, who wasn't taking the matter quite as easily as Callum. "There are advantages to not being chief. I can do as I wish, and Ranald can disavow my actions."

Charlie knew this was not nearly as simple as Callum was making it, but he was a loyal friend for whom Charlie was grateful. The four of them would do anything for one another—or for the women they loved. It was a simple pact—never expressed—but understood just the same.

THEY CAMPED for the night on a hill overlooking the castle. It was still light enough to see that the MacQuarries had stopped their attack on the castle, for now.

Callum studied the slope to the shore from the castle. "They're starving them out."

"Can they do it?" asked Alex. "Have they a good store of food?"

"I didnae see what they had, other than what was on the table," Charlie said. "Had I known I would need to—"

"Relax, lad. We're only trying to determine their state so we ken what to do next."

Charlie gave Callum an apologetic nod.

"Sometimes men grow weary." Duncan studied the MacQuarrie camp. "If they're weary enough, they might be ready to negotiate."

"Negotiate? How, when we've nothing to offer?" Callum's brows drew together, but he kept his thoughts to himself.

Alex leaned forward, elbows on knees. "From what I can see, they've been here a week and not breached the gate. They know that the Privy Council has ruled against them. They've made a good effort, so their pride would survive unscathed if they were to go home."

"Aye, it does happen often enough," said Callum. "And you're thinking..."

Alex nodded.

"That with some encouragement..."

Alex finished the sentence. "They might give up."

Duncan eyed Callum. "Your word carries weight with Sir Murray."

Callum nodded. "Aye, well, we'll find that out in the morning."

Chapter 15

The View from the Ramparts

Dark clouds blew in from the sea. Alone and unmoving, the castle stood in defiance of the wild sea winds that bent the tops of the trees on the brae. The stonework had taken some blows. Dents and scars peppered the side that faced the MacQuarrie camp.

While Charlie and Alex went around to the other side of the castle in search of someone on the battlements who might recognize Charlie, Callum and Duncan rode down to the MacQuarrie encampment, which had just released a volley of arrows.

Once he and Duncan established themselves as friends rather than foes, they were taken to Sir Murray, who first ordered the archers to cease then turned to Callum. "And what brings you here?"

It was an obvious question, for which Callum had no ready answer. He was there by the grace of Sir Murray and the good terms they'd established in the past. Moreover, Callum's flawless reputation and commanding but calm manner put people at ease. Added to that, at his side was a tall, dark, imposing companion, who looked as though he would give back whatever was given, and then some by half.

"What goes on here?" Callum asked quietly.

"My family has a prior claim on this land."

"Centuries ago."

"That doesnae make it any less of a claim."

"Sir Murray, listen to me. You're setting yourself against the Privy Council. Do you really wish to argue your case out of court like this?"

Sir Murray looked frankly at him. "Her brother brought this upon himself."

"Her brother isnae here."

"No, because he's"—Sir Murray smiled to himself—" a guest in my keep."

Callum allowed a quiet moment, during which he hoped Sir Murray would reconsider. "Do you ken what will happen when the Privy Council learns that you've gone against their decision?"

"After I've recaptured the castle, I doubt they'll have overmuch to say about it." He let out a slight arrogant laugh that drew a harsh glance from Duncan.

Callum barely contained his distaste for the man. "By the Rood, I wouldnae be certain of that. As you must know, in such cases, the Privy Council has been known to issue letters of Fire and Sword against the offending party —that would be you. Are you sure that you're ready for that? For you'd not only lose this castle, but also your own. And you could lose your life."

"I just want what's rightfully mine."

"Aye, I can understand that. But sometimes, we must give up that which is rightfully ours in order to save what we've already got." Callum could not help but recall how, in one of the most difficult moments of his life, he'd given up his own castle, his land, and the chiefdom of his people. Such things were never easy, but sometimes, they were right and therefore needed to be done.

Sir Murray looked away and let out a deep sigh then gave Callum a questioning look. "Do you ken what you're asking?"

"I do."

A long moment passed.

Callum looked at the castle. Despite some new broken and fallen rocks, it stood strong. Sir Murray could leave now, save face, and in time, smooth things over with Isobel and her brother. It made sense, and he could see that Sir Murray was taking some time to consider just that.

"No." He shook his head as though he were convincing himself. "No, I'll not be beaten by a woman."

"A woman whose castle is strong," Callum said quietly.

His anger renewed, Sir Murray shook his head vehemently. "I'm sorry, Callum. I respect what you say, but I must see this through." He turned and began shouting orders.

The archers resumed shooting, while the men manning the battering ram moved it into position in front of the portcullis.

WITH CAULDRONS of boiling water at the ready, Isobel

shouted down to the MacQuarries. "Have you come back to bathe? We can smell you up here!"

MacQuarrie's men scrambled to escape the scalding water that rained down on them. Their efforts thwarted, the men returned to camp to regroup.

Isobel turned to Roddy and the others, who were laughing at what she had said. "Be wary."

"Fire!" cried a voice from the opposite corner of the castle. Smoke rose from below. Isobel cursed.

"I'll gather some folk to get water," Roddy said.

Isobel put a hand on his arm. "No."

Roddy peered at her from beneath the long strands of brown hair that touched his eyebrows. "But my lady, the fire!"

She leaned closer. "I filled the last bucket of water myself," she said quietly. "There's more mud than water left in that well. Dinnae let the others see. They'll lose heart."

Roddy's eyes widened.

Isobel looked down at the fire. The MacQuarries had left it to burn. She called to the nearest strong-bodied man. "Gather a half dozen with shovels to go outside and throw dirt on the fire."

"My lady. My lady!" Roddy scurried ahead, putting himself in her path to get her attention. Then he looked to make sure no one would overhear. "I can get water."

She looked at him as though he were the fresh-faced young lad who had arrived a year ago, not the young man he was growing to be. "Oh, Roddy, really? A skin full of water will be of no help to us now."

"The laird, your brother, swore me to secrecy, but I think he'd forgive me for telling you now."

"What could he have told you that I didnae already ken?"

Roddy cast guilty eyes down. "There's a tunnel."

"What?"

"Aye. No one kens that it's there."

"But I've lived here all my life. If there were a secret passage, I would know."

"No, 'tis true. I've seen it myself."

"But neither John nor my father ever told me."

Roddy hesitated. "He said 'twas only for the men to know—in case we got attacked."

"Oh, did he? Brilliant. Perhaps I should just let him rot in that dungeon while his castle falls down around us, since I cannae seem to be trusted with knowledge that could save us in case we're attacked!" She exhaled and tried to regain her composure. "Is there anything else it might help me to know?" She scowled at Roddy, who shook his head.

"My lady, I'm sorry, but he said not to tell you. I could not disobey."

She forced a gentle smile and touched Roddy's shoulder. "It isn't your fault. But I will have words with my brother when next I see him."

Down below, the fire had been doused, and Isobel saw that the stonemason had already begun to shore up the weakened part of the wall. Satisfied with the progress, she turned and brushed her hands on her skirts. "Now, Roddy, why don't you show me this tunnel?"

Stopping first to get some empty waterskins, Roddy led Isobel into the laird's bedroom and across to a wall perpendicular to the outside wall. There, Roddy pressed a spot in the oak molding. The panel moved inward on a hinge. Isobel thought of how many times she'd been in this room and had never known it was there.

They went inside, where an iron torch, sconce, and a tinderbox hung on the wall. Roddy lit the torch and led the way down a narrow spiral staircase. When at last they reached the bottom, they found themselves in a chamber. From there, they followed a tunnel that was barely high enough to stand up in. At the end of the tunnel were more stairs, although not as many as before, which led up. At the top, they found themselves inside a domed chamber built completely of stacked stones, expertly placed with no mortar, which met in a point at the top.

Isobel looked about with wonder. "It's one of the brochs!"

Roddy smiled. "Aye, my lady. The doorway looks out at the loch, and behind you are trees. A stream runs through there on its way to the loch. I can start bringing water to fill up the cauldrons."

"You'll need help, but we cannae tell anyone."

Roddy shook his head. "No, I'll bring the water myself."

"I'll help when I can," Isobel said. "But if I'm absent for too long, folk will wonder."

Roddy ran his fingers through his hair. "It will take a good while, but I'll work as fast as I can."

"At the very least, we'll have water to drink if they try to starve us out."

Roddy grinned. "They'll not defeat us, my lady."

His confidence made her smile. For the first time since the siege began, Isobel truly believed it.

They went to the stream and filled the skins they'd brought with them. They were on their way back to the broch when they were grabbed from behind, mouths covered, and dragged into the woods. Isobel fought, jabbing her elbows and kicking her feet, but her captor was larger and stronger than she.

"Shh... Be quiet, or you'll bring every MacQuarrie in Scotland upon us."

Recognizing his voice, she relaxed, and he loosened his hand. "Charlie?" She heard Roddy still struggling. "It's all right, Roddy. It's Charlie."

"Oh, aye." Roddy glanced at the man who released him with a mixture of annoyance and embarrassment for having let Alex get the best of him. But in the man's defense, he was powerfully built.

Charlie smiled. "And this is Alex."

"You've both come from Glengarry?" Isobel asked.

"Four of us, actually. Callum and Duncan are elsewhere in search of MacQuarries."

"Forgive my asking, but why are you here? 'Tis lovely to see you, but why?"

"To help you." Charlie was grinning for no clear reason that Isobel could come up with, but it lightened her heart.

"I might ask you the same," Charlie said. "Why are you here? Your castle—over there—is under siege. How did you get away?"

Isobel's eyes darted to Roddy, who shrugged. He was no help. Was it really a good idea to tell someone else— two people, actually, and four eventually—where the secret castle entrance was, when her own brother had not thought her trustworthy enough to know?

She stammered. "I cannae tell you."

"We're sworn to secrecy," Roddy chimed in, not all that helpfully.

Isobel cast him a look of caution that she hoped would keep the boy from disclosing more.

Charlie and Alex exchanged a look, then they both looked at the broch from where the pair had emerged.

"Excuse me a moment." Alex turned and went into the broch.

Knowing that Alex would find the torch still on the sconce where Roddy had set it, and the door to the passage open, Isobel looked up at Charlie. "It's a secret passage into the castle. I only learned of it minutes ago. Apparently, my father and brother didnae trust such knowledge even to me, so I thought it wouldnae be right to tell you."

"And you haven't," Charlie said as Alex rejoined them.

"Our well's gone dry, so we came here for water," Isobel said. "I ought to get back."

"I'll come with you," Charlie said in haste. He turned to Alex. "Would you find Callum and Duncan and tell them where we are?"

When Alex stared at him and lifted a brow, Charlie scowled.

This brought a smile from Alex. Or was it a smirk? While Isobel was deciding, Charlie touched her elbow and nodded toward the broch.

Although a light, courteous touch should mean nothing, it felt like everything to Isobel. Roddy followed, although Isobel was so acutely aware of Charlie, she nearly lost track of the lad.

By the time the trio emerged from John's secret passage, they'd formed an excuse for Charlie's arrival. He'd called up to Isobel from the ground, and she'd heard him and thrown down a rope. The fact that she had no such rope long enough was a detail they hoped would slip by everyone's notice.

"As far as anyone knows, I could spend all of my evenings spinning, twisting, and winding ropes. How do they know I don't have a wardrobe full of them?"

"I've no doubt you could do anything you chose to." Charlie was smiling again, and Isobel realized that she was smiling as well.

They made haste to the ramparts to see how their defense fared. For most of the afternoon, the MacQuarries had stayed in their camp.

"What are they up to?" Isobel asked.

CALLUM AND DUNCAN rode back from the camp to their designated meeting spot up in the hills.

"God, that MacQuarrie needs to bed a woman—and soon," Duncan said.

Callum laughed. "He's a bit highly strung."

But Duncan insisted. "Half the world's problems would be solved by the love of a good woman. Failing that, a bad woman would do."

"I doubt that Sir Murray would ken the difference."

They arrived to find Alex sitting and leaning back against a tree. "How was the parley?" he asked.

"He'll not be defeated by a woman," Callum said.

Duncan sank down beside Alex. "But that woman could conquer that arse. 'Tis only a matter of time."

Callum glanced about. "And where's Charlie?"

"By now, he's in that castle somewhere with his lady love," Alex said. "God, that man's got second sight where women are concerned. He just finds them—or rather, they just find him. If I weren't so happily married, I'd hate him."

IT WAS the time of evening when the last light lingered, reluctant, in the sky and the distant hills faded until they resembled inverted clouds for a time. Soon, the darkness would come, and the sky would hover, quiet and vast. There would be no more attacks for the night.

Charlie took Isobel's hand and led her up to the ramparts. "You've done well—better, I daresay, than your brother would have." He stared into the distance. "I came here to help, but you dinnae need me."

Isobel felt proud of what she and her people had done. "Perhaps not in that way."

He turned and gave her a piercing look. "If things were different..."

Her breath caught in her throat. "What things?"

He looked down and shook his head. "You deserve—"

The words he had once spoken still rang in her ears. "To be loved. So you've said." Then something inside her erupted. "I don't want to deserve! I just want—" *To be loved.* At least she hadn't said it. She exhaled and gave her head a slight shake, then started to turn away.

He stepped forward and reached out, slipping his fingers up the nape of her neck, through her hair, and he kissed her. He kissed her until her head swam. She sank into his chest and clung to him, knowing that if she let go, she might never again feel his touch or his lips against hers.

But he pulled away gently. "If I could, I would hold you and never let go." Even as he said it, his hands grasped her shoulders, and he took a step back.

"Such a useless word, *if*. So often followed by words that are empty."

He looked as though he wanted to contradict her, but he could not. The same hands that had pushed her away still held her shoulders as if they could not let go.

Nor could she pull herself free of their strength or their warmth. Each moment he held her was breaking her heart, but she accepted her fate for as long as he would hold her. She was a lady—a strong lady, who had defended her castle, but one who could not seem to defend her own heart.

She lifted her eyes to look into the blue depths of Charlie's once more, then she fled.

"Isobel!"

She ran down to her chamber, pushed the latch into place, and stared at the door. "If I could, I would hate you for making me love you."

No one defending the castle ate at the table anymore. Food was brought to the ramparts and eaten if and when people were able. The MacQuarrie camp was awake and moving about.

Charlie joined Isobel, watching the MacQuarries' movements. His brow creased as he failed to think of anything to say that would make her feel better—or him, for that matter. They both knew how impossible things were for them. With her brother, the laird, captured and locked in the MacQuarrie dungeon, it would take a great deal for Charlie to establish his strength among clans in the region.

Any scandal—like having his sister run off with a crofter—would just make matters worse for not only John, but for his clan... and for Isobel. She would be disgraced—never able to return to her home.

How would Charlie be able to make up for that? At first, they might be happy together, but when the newness wore off, there would be no escaping the truth. He would have ruined her life, and ruined her in the bargain.

She spoke as if nothing had happened between them. "They're preparing for something."

He nodded then stole a glance at her.

One of the crofters stopped before her, catching his breath. "My lady! Three men broke into the castle!"

"Three men?" Charlie asked. "What did they look like? Where are they?"

Another crofter answered. "We tried to stop them, but—"

"Charlie, would you tell these fine folk who we are."

One man had a shovel raised over Alex's head.

"Stop!" cried Isobel. "He's a friend! He's here to help us!"

The crofter lowered his shovel. "Well, he shouldnae barge into castles without being invited," he grumbled.

"Aye, but I imagine he had little choice," Isobel said kindly. "Thank you for guarding us, Donald."

Still frowning, Donald gave her a nod and left.

Callum apologized to Isobel then asked what he could do.

She met his gaze frankly. "We've no warriors to fight them, so we're holding our ground and hoping that they'll grow weary and give up before they've ruined the castle they so desperately want."

He nodded.

"Unless you can think of a better plan," Isobel added.

"No, I have faith in Sir Murray to fail," Callum said with a glint in his eye. "Give him time."

Still, as Charlie watched the MacQuarries gather weapons and ropes, he decided it was time to speed things along. They had failed at undermining and battering rams, so it appeared they were planning to scale the wall, no doubt after using the trebuchet that stood idly next to the woods behind them. Charlie gestured to Duncan. The two had quiet words together.

The castle inhabitants crouched behind the wall as the usual volley of arrows whizzed by to announce the attack that would follow. At least Sir Murray MacQuarrie was consistent. He and his clansmen either had terrible aim, or they were aiming to intimidate rather than wound. In fact, there had been few injuries and no deaths—on either side, as far as Charlie could tell. Still, after more than a week, MacQuarrie had to be thinking of escalating his efforts to end the stalemate.

Charlie and Duncan climbed up to the ramparts and rounded a corner, where they nearly ran right into Callum and Alex. "Where have you two been?" Alex asked, looking annoyed.

Charlie looked at Duncan and shrugged. "Sawing logs."

"For wood fires?" Callum asked. "I'd rather we leave that to the crofters. We've too few seasoned warriors here as it is. I need you all here by my side."

"Aye, Callum," Charlie said.

"Aye," Duncan echoed as he and Charlie glanced at one another.

A number of men from the MacQuarrie clan headed for the trebuchet.

Isobel spoke without taking her eyes from the war machine. "I don't know how much more of that the castle can withstand."

"You'd be surprised," Duncan said.

Charlie elbowed him in the ribs. Seeing this, Callum's brow furrowed as he studied the pair.

Now in place, the trebuchet was readied. The long arm of the trebuchet was pulled down, which raised the counterweight. It remained in that position while they loaded a boulder into the sling. The men next released the long arm with the boulder, but the arm snapped off, leaving the boulder to fall the remaining few feet to the ground.

Everyone gasped then exhaled in relief. Callum stared at the trebuchet. "Hmm. Looks like a very clean break. Almost as if someone sawed it partway." He turned a skeptical look on Charlie and Duncan.

"Fancy that," Charlie said, working to maintain his expression.

Duncan slowly nodded. "Bad bit of luck for Sir Murray."

Callum and Alex exchanged looks then grinned at Charlie and Duncan, who both managed to shrug at the same time. That made everyone laugh, but their mirth was short-lived.

The MacQuarries were now firing arrows and scaling the wall. Having reached the wall under cover of dozens of arrows, the MacQuarries threw a rope over the top of the wall several times, until the grappling hook caught and held. Having been made a fool by the trebuchet incident, an enraged Murray MacQuarrie took the lead. As he rounded the top, he was met with four stern MacDonells, swords drawn, glaring at him.

"God's bones! MacDonell?" Surprised to see Callum, not to mention three more fierce MacDonell warriors, the man simply stopped there and clung to his rope.

"Would you care to rethink this?" Callum asked.

Sir Murray, not being in the best physical condition, did not take long to consider. "I've no quarrel with you!"

"Good, then perhaps it is time you go home," Callum calmly said. "Otherwise, it may not go well for you."

Sir Murray's face reddened. If he had any hope of making it over the top, he would never prevail over the four MacDonell men. Either from rage over his present defeat, or from the strain of hanging onto the rope for so long, he barked over his shoulder for the men below to climb down off the rope.

After MacQuarrie and his men had retreated and disappeared into the trees, a rifle shot rang out.

"What the devil?" asked Callum as they all ducked down for cover.

"Are you all right?" Charlie reached for Isobel, but Callum called to him from the opposite direction.

"Aye," she said softly.

"Charlie, stay here with Isobel," Callum said. "Alex and Duncan, come with me."

Charlie put a protective hand on Isobel's shoulder to keep her safely below the top of the wall, then he glanced back as his three friends disappeared down the tower stairs. With Isobel safe, he scanned the grounds for the shooter. All he saw were MacQuarries routinely breaking down camp and preparing to leave.

Charlie thought of the anger in Sir Murray's face as he was forced to accept his defeat. "God's wounds, the man doesnae know when to quit." He turned to find her slumped over. "Isobel!"

Thinking she'd fainted, he lifted her up to a sitting position. Warm blood soaked through her jacket and onto his hands. A moan came from her throat as he scooped her up into his arms and carried her down to her bedchamber, shouting orders to people he passed to bring water, bandages, and whisky.

He laid her down gently and tore away the clothing that covered the wound. She'd been shot in the shoulder. He had seen too many such wounds treated in battle. Turning her gently, he found an exit wound then laid her back down. He'd begun tearing strips of sheeting to bandage her. Someone handed a flask of whisky to him. He barely looked up. Taking it, he poured it into both wounds.

She moaned and opened her eyes. "You're hurting me!"

"I know, dearie," he said without looking up from his work. "But you've been shot, and I must dress your wounds." He wrapped the bandages over her shoulder.

When he was finished, he gently laid her down on the pillow to rest.

"Charlie?"

He tenderly smoothed strands of hair from her forehead. "Aye, I'm here, dearie. Get some sleep. I'll be here when you wake."

Her eyes drifted closed as he kissed her forehead. While she slept, Charlie leaned his elbows on the bed and buried his face in his hands. Why couldn't he have been shot? But he wouldn't have because the shooter must have been aiming for her. That bastard, Sir Murray. No one else would have done it. He dared not leave Isobel's side, or he would go after the man in an instant. But he would avenge this senseless shooting.

The next morning, Charlie lay sleeping in the chair beside Isobel's bed.

"Charlie."

He bolted upright and leaned over to her. "What is it, dearie?"

"May I please have some water?"

"Of course." He filled a glass from the pitcher and brought it to her. He lifted her head to help her drink. The back of her neck was alarmingly hot. When she'd finished drinking, he felt her flushed cheeks and her forehead. While she drifted to sleep, Charlie pressed cool, wet rags to her forehead. He prayed she would do better than so many men he had seen in a similar state.

For all of his life, Charlie had tempted fate. He'd enjoyed life and plenty of women, and he'd run head-on into danger. Other men faced fear in battle, but Charlie craved how it felt to fight enemy soldiers and come out the victor. Being close to death made him feel alive in a way he hadn't felt since his brother had died. He wasn't brave. He just wanted to feel—anything except aching grief. He'd been running from that since he'd left Edinburgh. But one day, he'd woken up in a barkeeper's byre, where he'd been left to sleep off too much drink. For a brief moment before he'd awoken, he'd dreamed he was home. And he had to go back.

It was only then that he found what he'd wandered the world in search of: peace with himself and someone to love. Perhaps he needed one in order to find the other. He didn't know. All he cared about was that somewhere along the way home, he had found the one woman who made him complete. He would watch over her now, and God help the man who had harmed her.

Chapter 16

The Admission

Isobel thrashed about and mumbled words that made no sense. She was burning with fever. Women from the village came in and tended to her, but it was Charlie who stayed with her through the dark hours of the night, and he was there when the sun rose for all except her. He wiped beads of sweat from her brow with wet rags and threw open the window to let in the cool Highland air. When she shivered, he held her.

It was during one of these moments that Callum came in and found Charlie holding a feverish Isobel. Behind Callum were Duncan and Alex, who both exchanged looks. When she grew calm again, Callum took Charlie out for some air.

"But I promised I'd be there when she awoke."

"And you will. Alex and Duncan are there, and they'll come get us if anything changes."

Charlie's face held a hollow expression. "I can't lose her."

Callum nodded. Charlie knew as well as Callum that there was nothing to say. Isobel was in danger of losing this battle. They could do nothing for her but wait.

Callum turned to a matter that could be addressed. "We spoke to everyone in the castle. No one saw who did it. Duncan and Alex are sure it was MacQuarrie, and I cannae disagree, but we have no proof."

Bitterness shone in Charlie's eyes. He needed no proof, but he would bide his time. Isobel needed him now.

CALLUM, Alex, and Duncan were on their way at sunrise to demand the release of the prisoners and to question Sir Murray about the shooting, when they came upon the men of Dernebroch on foot.

Sir Murray had released them upon his return home and had sent them home on foot. When asked about their horses, he'd said, "That's fair recompense for your food and lodging."

Callum told John about his sister. John's face grew taut. "Leave him. I'll see that he pays."

Callum saw the spite in the man's eyes and decided that waiting was better than having him strike out in a murderous rage, only to pay for it later at the end of a rope. If Isobel survived, she would need her brother, as would Clan McLeod. For now, their attentions were best focused on keeping Isobel safe in her home to recover. So they returned to Dernebroch, leaving the matter of Sir Murray for later. After washing the stench of the dungeon away, John went to his sister and found her in a fitful sleep with Charlie at her side.

"What are you doing in my sister's bedchamber?"

Charlie looked at him calmly. "Caring for her."

"Caring for her? And where were you when she was shot? Were you caring for her instead of protecting her?"

Charlie leapt to his feet, knocking over his chair in the process, and lunged for John. Callum stepped between them while Duncan grabbed hold of Charlie and pulled him away. Alex stood in John's way and urged him toward the hallway.

"I'll see my sister first."

Duncan spoke to Charlie quietly. "Leave him. It's his sister. Would you not do the same?" Charlie calmed down enough to walk out of the chamber with Duncan. Callum and Alex soon followed.

"There's no point in stirring up hard feelings now," Alex said. "The man's been locked up for more than a week."

Callum nodded. "Anything that you two need to talk of can wait until he—and his sister—are feeling better."

So Charlie waited until John had left Isobel's room, then he returned to her side. He would be there when she awoke, as he had promised.

A feast was prepared for the men who'd returned, and to thank all who had fought against the MacQuarries. It would have been bad form for the MacDonells not to go, but they quietly voiced their concern to one another that the celebration might be premature. But John was determined to eat and drink what he'd missed while confined in the dungeon. By the time three of the MacDonells arrived in the hall, John was so far into his cups that they doubted he would even notice Charlie's absence, so they chose to make no mention of it unless asked.

Before long, the homecoming celebration grew boisterous, and someone cursed MacQuarrie for what he'd done to Isobel.

John vowed to avenge her and see her safely married.

"In the meantime," said one of his hunting friends, "she's got Charlie MacDonell to keep her entertained." He raised an eyebrow. "That lass wasted no time."

A fist came from nowhere, grabbed the man by the neck, and pulled him up out of his chair. Charlie glared at the man who now looked up in fear. "Say what you want about me, but you mention the lady again, and I'll take pleasure in making you regret it."

The man nodded, and Charlie released him.

Charlie eyed John. "I left your sister's sickbed out of respect to you, to apologize for my earlier actions. Now, if you'll excuse me." He bowed politely and turned to leave.

As the merriment and chatter resumed, John frowned for a moment. "My God, you're in love with my sister." He took another drink of ale.

Charlie stopped and pivoted back to face John. "Aye."

John eyed Callum sternly. "Did you ken this?"

"I did," Callum said calmly.

John made no effort to look anything but displeased. "And you did nothing?"

Callum kept his gaze steady and focused on John. "I've known Charlie since we were bairns. He's a good man."

"Good for him." John shrugged. "But I have plans for my sister."

Charlie's jaw muscles twitched. "Perhaps you'd best wait to make plans until she's recovered."

John raised a brow. "I suggest you do the same."

Charlie flinched. Duncan gripped Charlie's shoulder and pressed him toward the door. Casting a dark look at John, Charlie turned and left with Duncan.

Chapter 17

The Chivalrous Knight

In the dark of night, Isobel was feverish and fitful. The MacDonell men had grown quiet and somber. Charlie wanted to shake them and insist she was not going to die, but he couldn't. He simply refused to acknowledge how close she was to leaving them all. If he admitted it, it somehow might happen.

"Charlie, get some sleep," Alex said. "We'll take turns sitting with her."

"Thank you, but no."

Alex hesitated, then he and the others left.

A few hours later, shadows flickered on the wall as the candle burned out. Charlie sat slumped in a chair by Isobel's bed with his head beside hers. With a start, he awoke from his short rest, distraught and exhausted. She was resting quietly for now, so he went to the window. Summer sun already lightened the sky, even though it was hours before anyone else would arise. Charlie opened the window and stared out at the sea and the sky above it.

"God in heaven, I dinnae deserve her, but she deserves to live. Even if she cannae be mine."

"Who are you talking to, Charlie?"

He turned to find her awake. He rushed over and sat beside her, stroking her forehead and cheeks. They were cool. Her fever had broken. It was all he could do not to weep, but he summoned his habitual charm and managed to smile. "I was just waiting for you to wake up."

"Were you?" she asked weakly.

He held her hand in both of his. "I told you I'd be here when you woke."

"You've been here with me all the while?"

"Aye, well, if you havenae noticed, I'm fair taken with you."

He pressed his lips to her hand and held it to his cheek as she drifted back to sleep.

ISOBEL GREW STRONGER in the days that followed. With the crisis passed, the MacDonells went home, all except Charlie. One afternoon, Isobel lay propped up on pillows and looked at the sun streaming in through the window. "Please, let me out of this room!" she said with a great sigh.

Charlie smiled, understanding yet knowing that she was in no way ready to make her way down the narrow stone spiral staircase. "Let's see what we can do." He got up and left her staring at the empty doorway. Minutes later, he was back with a book from the castle library. While the books seemed wasted on John, their father had amassed a fine library. Charlie's enthusiasm was infectious. "Madam, we are going to Spain," he announced.

Isobel grinned. "Spain? Lovely. I can almost feel the warm sunshine. And whom shall we meet there?"

"Ah, you're about to go on a journey with a noble and chivalrous knight."

Her eyes danced. "Oh, so it's a journey with you."

"Oh, aye, absolutely. And also another noble and chivalrous knight named Don Quixote."

He read to her, short passages at first, then more each day. They would talk about what they had read, and sometimes, Charlie would talk of the places he'd been. When Isobel longed for the sun, he carried her to the window seat and read to her there while she gazed out at the Isle of Skye and the sea beyond it. Before long, they were taking short strolls about the bailey. When they walked through the gates to the heath beyond, they both knew she was well.

On one such day, dark morning clouds had glided away, leaving a clear azure sky. They could not possibly ignore such a glorious day, so out they went. They'd been walking in comfortable silence, her arm in his, when Charlie said, "Look how well you manage without me."

"I do." Her eyes flitted toward his then lowered. "In most ways."

They both realized what this meant. Although they had avoided the topic, Charlie would be expected to leave now that Isobel had recovered. While her brother had been pleased to have someone take the burden from him for his sister's recovery, it was not an unending welcome. John had even come to accept Charlie's feelings for his sister, but he would not accept any talk of a future.

Charlie put his hand over hers. "I wish things were different."

"I like things just as they are at this moment."

Charlie averted his eyes. "Moments pass."

"Yes." Her smile faded. "I suppose that they must." She slipped her arm from his and pretended to brush some hair from her face, rather than directly swiping the tears from her eyes.

He struggled with whether to make a clean cut that would sting, or to open his heart for one instant of joy at the cost of the agony that would follow. "I wish..."

"Do you?"

The aching hope in her eyes was too hard to look at, so he looked off in the distance. "Some wishes are better left unsaid."

"I used to believe things like that."

He turned to her. "If I were someone else—"

"Then I wouldn't care. I wouldn't care about wishes —unless they were yours."

She looked pleadingly into his eyes, but he could only return stabbing regret. He took her hands in his. "Our lives crossed by chance. Any time that we've had was a gift."

"A gift?" She spoke softly, but anger burned through her tears. "How can feeling like this be a gift?"

"Must I say it? There is no future for us. I could no longer live here than you could in my croft."

She began to protest, but he stopped her. "You're the practical one." He tried to force a smile but failed. "When you've had time to think, you'll know that I'm right."

"I see." She searched his eyes, and he could not hide what she sought. Her brow furrowed. "Was I so mistaken?

I thought that you cared... more." She lowered her eyes, but the pain was still there.

A breeze blew wisps of Isobel's hair. Charlie smoothed it back and tilted her head up to gaze into her eyes. "You must know that I could not care more. I cannot care more." Instinct told him to leave it at that, but he could not leave her thinking he'd toyed with her feelings. The words spilled out. "I love you."

A tiny cry came from her throat.

He watched the breeze blow through the leaves of an oak. "I have tried to hold my feelings in check for a very long time. I thought if I didn't say the words, it wouldn't hurt quite as much. I was wrong. It hurts either way."

She started toward him, but as much as he wanted her in his arms, he shook his head and put gentle hands on her shoulders, keeping his distance. "I am a crofter's son. I come from good people. I would never change that. Nor would I change who I am—except that it keeps me from you."

"I would never ask you to change!"

His eyes softened as he looked at her. "Fine ladies who live in castles do not marry crofters."

"I dinnae care what fine ladies do!"

"But you are a fine lady, and you cannot change that any more than I can change who I am."

"I'm finished with being a lady, and doing my duty, and hiding my feelings!" She sank into his arms.

Charlie gave in and held her in his arms. "Whatever happens... whoever you marry—"

She looked up and shook her head in protest, but Charlie went on.

"I want you to remember that once you were loved—truly loved."

Isobel searched his eyes, and he kissed her. With all the love that consumed him, he kissed her once more, and they stood on the heath as the wind tossed the leaves and bent over the grasses. They clung to one another with all the love and desperation they shared.

He held her in his arms and cradled her head in his hand. "God help me, I can't leave you yet."

They put off his leaving, instead choosing to dream as if they could make dreams come true. All that mattered was love. So they resolved to steal each day from fate for as long as they could, knowing fate was neither patient nor forgiving of debts. In time, there would be a price.

Chapter 18

A Dram and a Blether

The next evening, Charlie went out for a ride and arrived at an inn where MacQuarries were known to gather. He'd been there once before, and he'd charmed the barmaid into telling him when Sir Murray liked to come by for a dram and a blether.

Not long after Charlie's arrival, Sir Murray dismounted and left his horse with the stableboy. He'd had a few not-so-wee drams when Charlie's fierce hand forced his face to the bar with a thud. "Back away!" he ordered the other men at the bar.

MacQuarrie groaned as Charlie bent down close and looked him in the eye. "You're alive now because she is. Had she not survived, you'd have met the same fate. I'd kill you just the same, but I'll not have her put through a scandal." Charlie gripped Sir Murray's chin and pulled him up, nearly out of the stool. His voice was quiet but menacing. "But if anything happens to that lady, I will come back. And when I do, you will wish you were already dead." With a shove, Charlie released him and left.

He was just about to mount his horse when he heard the soft snap of a flintlock being cocked. "How dare you come onto my land and threaten me."

Charlie stood still. "You'd shoot a man in the back, Sir Murray? At least let me turn to face you." Charlie raised his hand and turned slowly. His other arm came into view, as did the pistol he was holding. Charlie fired, and MacQuarrie fell.

Charlie walked over and looked down at the dying Sir Murray. "You fool. Did you think I'd not have a pistol at the ready?"

The door opened, and people spilled out from the pub just as Charlie leapt onto his horse and rode away.

A LOUD KNOCK on the solar door startled Isobel from her musings.

"Come in." Expecting a servant, her face lit up when she saw Charlie. Her smile faded when he strode in and quickly looked out the window then paced about, agitated.

"Isobel."

"Aye? What is it?"

His wild eyes and manner alarmed her. He led her to a chair then pulled another over to face her. He sat and took hold of her hands. "I had to see you—to tell you what's happened. You'll know the truth from me before the lies start."

He laid out the bare facts of what had happened.

"But you were defending yourself," she protested.

"Aye, but the only witnesses are MacQuarries, and you can be sure that their version will differ."

"Oh, Charlie!" Much as she wished to, she could not deny he was right.

He voiced what she feared. "They'll hang me for murder."

"But if it was self-defense, surely a judge will see that."

Charlie leveled a frank look. "Do you really believe they would bother to wait for a trial?"

She wanted to believe that good could prevail, but she knew the MacQuarries. "Where will you go?"

"Home—but only long enough to make arrangements."

"Arrangements?" Until now, she had clung to a thin thread of hope that the two of them could be together, but she now realized she was about to lose him forever. Before she could face him, she turned away and tried to pull her ragged emotions together. "You'll have to go far away," she whispered.

He put a gentle hand on her shoulder and gave it a squeeze. "Aye."

She gave a barely perceptible nod.

"I've upset you. I'm sorry."

"Upset me?" She shook her head and turned to him. "I have fought back against rifles, arrows, fires, and battering rams. I've had boulders hurled at my castle. I've seen my brother and his men returned from a dungeon to their homes and their families, and made sure they were safe. I did this—not because I am strong or brave, but because it was my duty to my family and my clan—the people I love. That upset me, but I did it."

Charlie's brow creased with pain.

She looked at him plainly. "And when you and your clansmen came to help me, you rode in and stood on the ramparts and looked at MacQuarrie. You just stood there and looked at him. That's all you did! And you won!"

"Oh, lass. When Callum met with Sir Murray, the man was half done with this then. But he wouldnae lose to a woman."

"Och, men! Sometimes I hate you all!" She angrily wiped a tear from her cheek. "Whether to a man or a woman, he lost. It was over. And throughout the siege—and since I met you at some point before that—there has only been one thing I've wanted for myself." She turned with fiery regret in her eyes. "To be loved. And you said I deserved it."

Frustrated, she stood and went to the window. "Why did you have to go see him?"

"Because he hurt the woman I love."

Isobel couldn't breathe for a moment.

"I nearly lost you," he said softly.

She could not turn to face him. "And now you will."

Charlie stood in pained silence.

"Yes, you've upset me," she said softly. "And I dinnae ken what to do." Isobel was too stunned to know that her heart had just broken. She only knew she was no longer whole. When she was able to turn and face him, she saw the same heartache in his eyes. She could not afford to be angry right now with so little time left. "Charlie!" She rushed to him, and he clutched her against him.

His lips were on hers, and her head swam with the joy of his touch, and the sorrow of knowing she would soon lose it.

He tore himself away. "I must go."

"I'll go with you."

"No. It's too dangerous."

"I'm good with a pistol."

He smiled. "So I've seen. But you'd have to use it on me before I'd put you in such danger."

Her eyes brightened. "Let's run away where no one knows us."

"And be exiled from our homes and our families— living in fear of discovery? And what if I'm found?"

She turned away, but he gripped her shoulders and forced her to look at him. "I could be taken and hanged for my crime, and then where would you be? All alone, with no home to return to?"

She shook her head but was helpless to argue against him.

"I must know that you're safe. And I'll be safer alone."

Of course he was right. He'd spent years as a soldier. Alex had told her that Charlie's skill with horses and weapons was unmatched. It hurt to admit he would be better off without her. She could endure it if she knew one thing. "Will I see you again?"

"Oh, my love." His eyes swept from her brow to her lips, and he kissed her. But he never answered her question.

Roddy knocked on the door and called out. "Charlie! I saw torches in the distance. They're coming for you!"

Charlie pressed one last kiss on Isobel's lips and threw open the door. "Thank you for keeping watch, lad."

"Shall I open the gate for you, sir?"

"Aye, lad. Let us make haste!"

He shot a piercing look back at Isobel. Then he was gone, down the stairs.

Chapter 19

Fate Comes Calling

Charlie burst into the dining room, where Callum, Duncan, Alex, and their wives all sat at breakfast.

He stopped and bowed his head to Mari. "Forgive me." He looked about and saw that the children were absent, no doubt up in the nursery. He'd known Kenna and Jenny since childhood, and had been through enough with Mari to feel he could speak frankly.

He turned to Callum. "Sir Murray is dead. I've killed him."

By the time he'd explained it, there was no doubt in anyone's mind that, despite having acted in self-defense, there would be no fair trial—and likely no trial at all.

Callum leaned forward. "The first place they'll look for you after Dernebroch Castle is here."

Alex agreed. "We should get you away before any MacQuarries come looking."

Charlie quickly nodded his agreement. "Aye. I ken that I cannae stay here."

"Come with me," Duncan said without hesitation.

"My sloop is docked near Fort William. We were planning to leave in three days. I'll send word to my crew to prepare for an early departure."

"We can be packed and ready to leave by the morning," Jenny said.

Alex shook his head. "That will just draw attention. You dinnae want talk in the pubs."

Callum nodded.

Duncan's eyes darkened. "True. Then we'll leave at the scheduled time." He turned to Jenny. "I'll leave with Charlie tonight. You and Hughie will follow later."

She nodded.

"I'll bring Jenny and Hughie there safely," Callum said.

Duncan looked at Charlie. "I'll hide you on the ship until we set sail."

Alex and Kenna whispered together, then Alex spoke up. "Callum, you've just had a bairn. Your wife needs you. I'll take Jenny and Hughie."

And so it was settled. Charlie and Duncan bade farewell and were off the next morning. They arrived after dark the next night and boarded the sixty-foot sloop.

Duncan lit a lantern and hung it from a hook in the rafter. It cast its light over a good-sized room with a large table in the center, which had several navigational charts strewn upon it. In one corner was a bunk, where Duncan slept—and, Charlie surmised, Duncan's wife, Jenny, when she traveled with him. It was a bit small for two people, but he imagined neither Duncan nor Jenny minded all that much. A single drawer from the bureau lay on the floor with a pillow inside it—no doubt for young Hughie. The floor was covered with a thick Persian carpet. Upon it

were scattered a few trunks and two barrels that func-
tioned as tables. Velvet curtains hung over a large window,
and the wall beside it held an impressive arsenal of
firearms.

"Just what sort of business are you in?" Charlie asked.

"A good business that's provided well for my family."

"So I see."

Duncan tossed a blanket to Charlie. "We'll talk more
in the morning."

Charlie made himself comfortable with a thick carpet
for a bed.

THE NEXT MORNING, bright sun shone through the
gaps in the curtains. Duncan was up, and a cabin boy
brought in a tray with breakfast. The table was set, and
the two men were left to their meal.

"Can the lad be trusted?" Charlie asked.

"Oh, aye. I found the lad on a ship we'd taken over.
He'd been kidnapped as a young boy. He had no home or
family that he knew of, so I've offered him work here until
he's old enough to foster with Callum or Alex. He'd be a
fool to betray me and give up a fine future. Besides which,
I trust him."

Charlie listened to the sounds of Duncan's crew
moving about and responding to orders. "It sounds like
quite a good-sized crew."

"Close to a hundred." Seeing Charlie's reaction,
Duncan grinned, clearly pleased with his life. "Aye." He
leaned forward conspiratorially. "We're privateers."

"You're a pirate?"

"Not quite. I've been commissioned by the crown, so it's all very legal."

Charlie looked about. "And you've made a fortune."

"A small one. Charlie, I could use some help."

"With all these men around you?"

Duncan looked up toward the source of the current voices at work. "They're good men, but I need someone I can trust. And there are only three people alive who can fit that description."

Charlie met Duncan's eyes and gave a nod, for he felt the same way.

"Give it some thought. I could teach you what you need to know. You already ken how to fight. It's the same here but on water."

Charlie laughed. "I somehow suspect that it's not quite that easy."

"I've my eye on a new ship. When you're ready, it could be yours to command. In a year or two, you could acquire your own small fortune. Come, Charlie, adventure awaits!" Duncan laughed.

Charlie looked at Duncan's bright eyes, and the thrill of a new adventure could not be denied. "Where do I sign?" he asked with a shrug.

DUNCAN AND CHARLIE went on great adventures and dangerous ones, though Duncan never shared those with Jenny. She knew of his escapades, nonetheless, for she'd dressed as a cabin boy and sailed with him until Hughie was born.

Now they lived a genteel life in a grand house near

Londonderry, where Duncan docked his ship every couple of months. This last journey, however, had taken Charlie and Duncan to Barbados. After three months, they pulled back into port and docked with a ship full of cargo to trade.

Duncan and Charlie went into a tavern and sat with a silk merchant they often did business with. The merchant was bent down, examining samples of silk, when a gentleman walked over and stopped at their table.

"MacDonell!" Duncan and Charlie both looked up. Murray MacQuarrie stood before them with a sly grin on his face.

Stunned, Charlie looked at the ghost, who appeared very much in the flesh.

"Oh yes, I'm alive. You did your best, but you didn't kill me." Sir Murray stood scowling with hatred and pride.

Charlie met MacQuarrie's cold gaze boldly. "I defended myself when you were about to shoot me in the back, if that's what you mean."

Sir Murray barely acknowledged Charlie's words. "It's taken some months to find you, but my men here got word of your friend, Duncan." Two men stood on either side of Sir Murray. "He's becoming quite a legend on the high seas. 'Twas said that he had a new partner. Oh, aye, Charlie. You're the talk of the taverns—at least among the working ladies. So dashing, they say. And here you are, at last."

Sir Murray drew a pistol. Having no time to load his own pistol, Charlie pulled his dirk and struck the man's wrist from underneath. The pistol flew into the air, where it discharged and took out a chunk of the rafter. This cleared the tavern in an instant, as people ducked and scrambled for the door.

Sir Murray drew his sword and swung at Charlie, but Duncan had already drawn his. While Duncan crossed swords with Sir Murray, Charlie hopped on the table and parried blow after blow from the two bodyguards. Duncan, meanwhile, had disarmed Sir Murray with one swipe of his sword, which sent Sir Murray's sword flying. In the moment that followed, Duncan thrust his dirk into one of Sir Murray's henchmen. The man staggered and sank to the floor.

Sir Murray retrieved his sword and came after Charlie. Duncan lunged for the remaining bodyguard, drawing his attention away, freeing Charlie to focus on Sir Murray.

Charlie's eyes narrowed, while the edge of his mouth hinted at a smile.

"Why, you cocky bastard." Temper flaring, Sir Murray swung out of anger, which cost him precision.

Charlie pulled back his sword and let his opponent's momentum pull him forward. This movement forced Sir Murray to take a small step to recover his balance. Charlie lifted his foot and gave Sir Murray a shove with his boot that sent him backward, arms flailing.

Landing on his back knocked the wind out of him. While he struggled to recover, Charlie stepped on Sir Murray's chest, pinning him down. He watched with approval as Duncan dispatched the second bodyguard, who now lay facedown over the bar. The startled barkeep emerged from hiding.

Duncan leaned his elbow on the bar. "I'll have a whisky—and another for my friend." He handed a bag of coins to the barkeep. "And this should take care of the damage."

Charlie glanced down to find Sir Murray's hand slipping a sgian dubh from his belt. With one swift move, Charlie kicked it out of his hand then pulled him to his feet by the collar. "Don't make me kill you again."

With one blow, Charlie knocked the man out. Sir Murray fell to the ground, and Charlie took a whisky from Duncan.

Both grinned. "Sláinte!" they said in unison.

CHARLIE BURST into the dining room with a document clutched in his hand. Duncan, Jenny, and Hughie looked up from their supper.

"Hello, Charlie," Duncan said with a smirk.

Charlie grinned. "I'm sorry. Sorry, Jenny, but I've a letter from Callum. He's been to Edinburgh."

"Aye?" Duncan's enthusiasm didn't seem to match Charlie's, but he was unfazed.

"I've two bits of news, one good and the other even better. Which shall I share first?" Charlie could not hide his joy.

Bemused, Duncan looked at Jenny, who shrugged. "The good news," she said.

"Callum has obtained—well, it's actually issued to Ranald, as he's Laird of Glengarry—a Commission of Fire and Sword against Murray MacQuarrie." Charlie began to read the decree.

"In light of his attempted seizure of Dernebroch

Castle and the attempted murder of the Lady therein, as well as two prior attempts..."

He paused, skipping to the important part. "Well, in short, we've the authority to...

"Search, take, and apprehend the above-named person, and to put them to the knowledge of any assize for the crimes aforesaid, and to administer justice upon them and execute them to the death; and, if need be, to raise fire and sword and to burn their houses and slay them in case they make opposition or resistance in the taking and apprehending."

"Sounds a bit thorough," Duncan said with a wry grin.

A crooked smile formed as Charlie's eyes lit. "Aye, well, I'm hoping that reading that might calm him down so the full extent of the commission need not be executed."

Duncan looked up at Charlie. "Sir Murray calm down? I doubt that."

"If the man insists upon dying, there's not much I can do. But he cannae be fool enough to fight this. Either way, 'tis good news for me."

"'Tis fine news!" Duncan smiled then glanced at Hughie, who, unaware of the grown-up matters about him, began talking to the imaginary woodland creatures in the garden rows he'd made of tatties and neeps on his plate. Duncan caught Jenny's eye, and they shared a warm look.

Charlie cleared his throat. "Do you not wish to hear the other news I've brought?"

"The even better news?" Jenny asked.

"What is it?" Duncan clapped his hands together.

"Have you finally decided to marry the lovely Mistress Shaw?"

That caught Charlie off guard. He shook his head as a flicker of sadness came to his eyes. "No." Then his face brightened. "The news is that while Callum was in Edinburgh, he heard of a certain dragoon who had overstepped his authority. The more he heard, the more intrigued he became, so he asked what the man's name was."

"Tavish MacLean," Jenny whispered.

Charlie grew somber. "It seems that a young soldier in MacLean's charge was locked up for a minor infraction and left without food or water for days. He nearly died. The rumor is that the young soldier was... well, let's call him an unacknowledged, but well-provided for, son of an influential earl. Whether that is true, no one can say. But shortly after the incident, Tavish MacLean was cashiered."

Duncan's expression clouded as he gave barely a nod.

"I don't understand," Jenny said.

"Before a parade ground assembly of troops, he was ceremonially stripped of his rank," Charlie said. "They knocked off his cap, broke his sword, and he's lost the right to get back the price of his commission."

"I'm not happy to hear it, but he deserved it," Duncan said.

Charlie's eyes settled on Duncan as he recalled all his friend had suffered under Tavish MacLean. "They say he couldnae live with the disgrace, so he went to the islands, where no one would know him."

Jenny slipped her hand into Duncan's. "I dinnae ken if I would call that even better news. Perhaps justice better describes it." Duncan nodded and went to the window. He stood pensively staring.

"I'm not done," Charlie said. "When Callum heard that, he contacted one of the prisoners he'd come to know well while in Covenanter's prison."

"Who?" Duncan asked. "I may know him from when I worked there as a guard."

"I asked him the same, but he was sworn to secrecy as to the man's identity for political reasons."

"I can understand that," Duncan said, looking troubled.

Charlie knew talk of MacLean would bring back memories his friend would rather have forgotten, but it couldn't be helped. He took a step closer to Duncan. "The main point is that as a result of Tavish's actions coming to light, he was able to get all charges against you dropped," Charlie said.

Jenny rushed to her husband.

Duncan held her in his arms. "We're going home."

Chapter 20

Frost on the Heath

"No, John, I'll not marry again." Isobel rose and went to the window.

"It's been over a year since the death of your husband."

Ignoring him, Isobel said nothing.

John tried again. "It would help mend the rift between our clans."

"But, John, the MacQuarries? Have you gone mad? Yes, you have. We'll not speak of it again."

John shrugged and sat down in his favorite chair in the solar, whisky in hand. "Very well, but it would be good for the clan."

She turned and walked slowly and deliberately toward her chair. Her voice was as sweet as honey when she spoke. "John, I was thinking. There are two or three of those MacQuarrie girls of marrying age. And you're such a braw, strapping lad. Perhaps *you* could marry one of them —for the sake of the clan." She smiled sweetly.

"Och! You're daft, woman."

Her eyes twinkled as she sat down to read. "Aye."

John heaved a sigh. "You used to be so agreeable—before you met him."

"Aye, I was, wasn't I? I rather like things this way."

"Well, marriage or not, 'tis time you got over him."

"Can you ever get over love? Love is a force all its own."

John eyed her with pity. "What's happened to you?"

"Love."

He shook his head. "You used to be so sensible."

"Love isn't sensible."

"Oh, Izzy, you're hopeless."

She smiled at him warmly. "I do hope so."

BRIGHT SUN SHONE down on the frost-covered heath —the same heath Isobel had walked with Charlie when summer was warm and grass shook in the wind. As much as she believed what she'd told John that morning, a twinge of doubt tormented her, as it had for some time. Murray MacQuarrie had survived. By the time he recovered, news of his encounter with Charlie had spread through the Highlands, to the point that Charlie was becoming a sort of folk hero.

With Sir Murray's survival, there were no murder charges against Charlie, leaving him free to come home. So why had he not come back to her? The same answer taunted her. He'd never promised to, had he?

She turned and started for home, pulling her airisaid close around her. The afternoon breeze had grown cold. Stepping through the broken grass, now brown and lifeless, she planned the rest of her day. It would be simple, like all of her days. But she had a good life, a fine home, and a warm fire that waited there for her.

Once inside, she heard loud voices from the solar. "You'll not get a halfpenny from me," her brother said.

"Oh, God help me, John's found me another suitor," she whispered. Whoever he was, she knew he had not come out of any affection for her. She did not possess the sort of unfathomable beauty or charm that would have motivated one to do so. Like others before him, the new suitor must have just wanted her dowry.

She stopped outside the door and listened.

"He doesnae need your money," a rich, dark voice said. "Nae doubt he's got more wealth than you."

Isobel sighed. *A rich one—and one who doesn't want my dowry? John won't be able to resist that. But then, what does this man want? He must be from a rival clan.*

A second voice spoke in a calm and pleasing tone. "We came here out of friendship for him—and for you, if you'll have it."

A third voice! Good lord, how many men does it take to propose?

"Look, John, we've done nothing but kindness for you—a damn sight more, truth be told."

Something about his words and the timbre of his voice drew her notice, but the heavy door muffled the sound. She stepped closer and stood mere inches from the door.

"I'd consider it a personal honor if you would forge a bond between our clans in this way," the second man said.

Isobel groaned. She could not listen to any more. As

she walked away, John said, "Och, can't you see? I'm just having some fun!"

She was halfway down the hall when the door flew open. Footsteps emerged but then stopped. "Isobel?"

She whirled around and gasped, too shocked to move.

"Charlie?" She could barely whisper his name.

He moved toward her, looking at her with soft blue eyes tinged with fear as he took her hand in both of his. "Marry me."

She stared at him as if she had not understood.

When she said nothing, he swallowed and took a deep breath. The poor man was undone. "I'm sorry I blurted it out. But I love you, and I—"

"Yes!"

"Want to spend my life with you—what?"

"Yes!" She was laughing through her tears.

"Yes?" His brow creased. "Are you sure?" He began to smile.

"Yes, I'm sure." She looked at the nervous man before her. "Are you?"

Calmness came over him. "Aye." Then he lifted her chin and kissed her, while his three friends and Isobel's brother gathered at the doorway.

Duncan gave them an approving smirk. "Good God, he's finally done it."

"It's a miracle," Callum said.

"That she'd have him?" Alex asked. "Oh, aye."

Duncan shook his head. "God! Imagine it, all of us married!"

Slowly, their gazes all turned to John.

Chapter 21

A Highland Oak

Summer came, and with it, a wedding. The Highlands were draped in rich greens, while gunmetal clouds with white cotton edges dipped down and brushed the hilltops. Summer grasses and flowers scented the air as Charlie and Isobel walked out of the chapel and the music began. Pipes, violins, a bodhrán, and voices all rose in song. By the time all the food was laid out on nearby tables, the clouds had given way to a clear azure sky.

It seemed everyone in the village had come to celebrate. The MacDonell men, their families, and the folk of Glengarry spread blankets about and sat basking in the treasured sunshine between dances. Alex and Kenna's Gillian played big sister to young Hughie, while Callum held Grace's hands as she aimlessly toddled. With a sigh, Mari looked about with a soft light in her eyes and sat down to join her family and friends. Duncan was in the midst of describing the house he was building for Jenny, which was not far away from the one Charlie was building. The four MacDonell men sat talking and laughing.

They were home now, building new lives and families and stories to tell.

Amid all the lively comings and goings, no one noticed Charlie take Isobel's hand and lead her behind a large oak. There, he swept her into his embrace and planted a daringly passionate kiss on her lips.

"Charlie!" She looked about, shocked to discover a white-haired couple walking past.

The man's arm was hooked though his wife's, giving her the support she needed to walk. With a twinkle in his eye, he looked over to Charlie and said, "Gie it laldy!"

The old woman whispered a scolding remark, but she smiled, nonetheless.

Charlie grinned and gave them a wave.

Isobel looked at him, puzzled. "What did he say?"

Charlie chuckled. "Give it your all. Like this, Mistress MacDonell." And he kissed her until she was fully aware of the meaning.

The Highland Soldiers Series

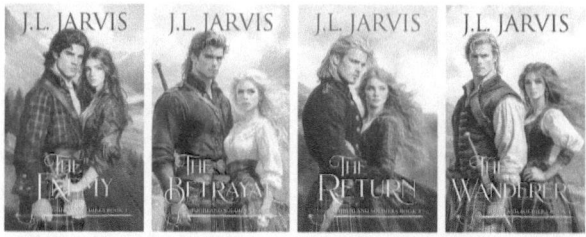

Highland Soldiers: Scottish historical romances set during turbulence seventeenth-century Scotland

Thank You!

Thank you for reading! If you enjoyed this book, please consider leaving a review or a rating. Your feedback on bookstore, Goodreads, and Bookbub websites helps other readers discover books they'll enjoy.

instagram.com/jljarvis.writer

facebook.com/jljarvis1writer

x.com/JLJarvis_writer

youtube.com/@jljarvis-author

goodreads.com/jljarvis

bookbub.com/authors/j-l-jarvis

Also by J.L. Jarvis

Waterfront Summers

(Can be read in any order)

The Cottage at Peregrine Cove

The House on Serenity Lake

Moonlight on Mariner's Bluff

Drake & Wilde Mysteries

(Reading Order)

Love in the Time of Pumpkins

Secrets in the Hollow

Shadow of the Horseman

Standalones

(Can be read in any order)

A Cowboy Kind of Love

A Christmas Eve Stop

Christmas by Lamplight

A Kiss in the Rain

App-ily Ever After

Once Upon a Winter

The Red Rose

Highland Vow

Short Stories

The Holiday Hideaway

Highland Passage

(Can be read in any order)

Highland Passage

Knight Errant

Lost Bride

Highland Soldiers

(Reading Order)

The Enemy

The Betrayal

The Return

The Wanderer

American Hearts

(Can be read in any order)

Secret Hearts

Forbidden Hearts

Runaway Hearts

For more information, visit jljarvis.com.

Get monthly book news at news.jljarvis.com.

About the Author

J.L. Jarvis is a left-handed former opera singer/teacher/lawyer who writes books. She now lives and writes on a mountaintop in upstate New York.

jljarvis.com

www.ingramcontent.com/pod-product-compliance
Lightning Source LLC
Chambersburg PA
CBHW020409210626
46816CB00006BB/2197